Smi X-SS
Smith, Julie,
Mean rooms

1st ed.

$ 21.95

MEAN ROOMS

MEAN ROOMS

Julie Smith

Five Star
Unity, Maine

Five Star Mystery
Published in conjunction with Tekno Books and Ed Gorman.

Cover photograph by Jason Johnson

March 2000

First Edition, Second Printing

Five Star Mystery Series.

The text of this edition is unabridged.

Set in 11 pt. Plantin by Rick Gundberg.

Printed in the United States on permanent paper.

Library of Congress Cataloging-in-Publication Data

Smith, Julie, 1944–
    Mean rooms : a short story collection / Julie Smith. — 1st ed.
    p. cm. — (Five Star standard print mystery series)
    ISBN 0-7862-2364-2 (hc : alk. paper)
    1. Detective and mystery stories, American. I. Title. II. Series.
PS3569.M537553 M4 2000
813'.54—dc21   99-056408

Table of Contents

Introduction

Years ago, I wrote an absolutely preposterous story and sent it to a friend with a note that said, "Barring one item, everything in this story actually happened."

Here was the plot of the story: Employees get together, much like the folks in *Murder on the Orient Express*, and kill their highly deserving boss by exotic, yet magnificently appropriate means.

My friend was quite sure he figured out the thing that wasn't true-some technicality involving what was meant to be an utterly fantastical murder method.

I still have trouble believing anyone could miss the point so entirely. The part that wasn't true was the entire plot! No employees I've ever heard of could possibly band together to murder their boss. But every maddening detail about what the boss put them through was gospel

This may say something about my approach to the short story—or perhaps about any writer's approach to any form of literature. Everything starts with a kernel of reality, and that kernel is the engine that drives the story; the point of the story, if your will—the tiny spark the author hopes will help to illuminate the human condition.

Everything else is just a *story*.

Some of the stories herein are satirical, and satire is always a way of nibbling at the truth. These are stories about our frustrations, and what we'd do about them if we could—old-fashioned revenge fantasies.

7

Some are inspired by people I've been unfortunate enough to meet or hear about—including one convicted murderer. Two are based on stories people have told me about their lives or other people's. I'd particularly like to mention *Where the Boys Are.* This one, if I heard my informant correctly, really is all true—plot, motivation, every single thing except one or two details. It's the only real-life story I've ever come across in which an amateur detective actually solves a crime. If I've been misinformed, I don't want to know about it. *Always Othello* comes from a remark a psychiatrist really made to me at a party.

These two stories don't take themselves too seriously, an attitude I sometimes enjoy in a short story, which can be a sort of literary shaggy dog tale, told purely for amusement. But even with a little levity here and there, I expect there are few stories in the collection that don't contain at least a suggestion of what I call "mean rooms."

Crime may happen on the mean streets, but criminals are forged indoors. Our dark sides awakened in claustrophobic spaces where the parent shames and beats the child. Once aroused, evil can grow and build upon itself, the rooms growing ever meaner. The wife humiliates the husband, the husband beats the wife, the merchant cheats the partner. If the rooms are nasty enough, the child sufficiently damaged, the spouse hurt badly enough, the meanness can spread to the streets. But that is some other writer's bailiwick.

Most of us have all we can handle coping with the indoors. A good yarn can take the pressure off.

Silk Strands

She looked at the clock. Eight-ten. Two hours before anyone who knew her habits ever called, much less rang her doorbell. What was going on? Even the UPS man never showed up till nine-thirty.

She sat up suddenly, remembering the events of the last couple of days. Dennis! He must have gotten so mad he'd come over to rant. She had a moment of doubt, a flash of fear, but that was all.

Pulling on a pair of sweats, she smiled to herself. Good. She wanted to see him rant, yell, really get down for once. She wanted to see his famous lack of affect replaced with purple rage. She wanted to see any emotion at all, even blind fury flow out of him, knowing it would make her feel less sad, less disconnected, less as if she'd just spent the winter at the North Pole.

A man and a woman stood on the threshold, the man holding up a badge. "Police. Are you Morgan Ellender?"

"Yes."

"You know a man named Dennis Hargett?"

God! She hadn't done anything illegal. How had he gotten them to do this? Harassment—that would be what he'd claimed. He'd probably actually gone to the police station and reported her. But they wouldn't be here if it weren't for the damned TV station. They'd undoubtedly come as a favor to him. She declined to be intimidated.

"I really don't have time to talk to you now." She looked at

9

her wrist as if she were wearing a watch. "I have to be some-where at nine."

"I'm afraid we have bad news for you, Miss Ellender. Mr. Hargett was shot last night."

The woman spoke: "I'm sorry, Miss Ellender. I'm afraid he's dead. We understand you were involved with him."

Oh, dear God! Dead was the last thing she wished him. She'd spent weeks trying to ferret out incipient signs of life, nourish them, fan them till they burst into flame, hoping to warm them once they'd become stranded together, two urban souls lost in a bewildering fog of hormones. And all he had done was freeze her with his already half-deadness. It wasn't she who had finished the job, but she knew why the cops were here.

She let them in, offered tea, and let them show her the pink message slip.

She had met him at a party given by a friend of a friend. She hadn't known many people there and had been surprised when the nice-looking man in glasses, the only man there wearing a tie, had spoken to her.

"Aren't you Morgan Ellender? I've heard you read."

That one was always a difficult beginning. Was she simply to smile expectantly, hoping for the crumb of praise that was often a poet's only pay?

"I hope you enjoyed it," she said.

He said, "I'm Dennis Hargett" and as they shook hands she felt a surge of energy between them. He was a big man, very preppy, not her usual type, but blond, and she had a weakness for blonds. Her last husband had been one.

"You look like Joan Baez," he said. "But everyone tells you that."

In fact, no one had in a long time. She had worn her hair

short for years, and then had lost most of it. In reaction, she had grown it long again, like the young Baez, and realized with pleasure that it was making the statement she wanted. Gradually, she had felt herself coming back, coming out of her shock and sadness, her vulnerability, and she wanted long, free-swinging hair as a symbol of her return to life.

Her husband had left—the third one, Gordon, the one whose bronze skin and gold hair had inspired fifty poems about precious metals, most of them unpublishable. She had fallen into what they had called a swoon in earlier centuries—a wounded withdrawal from life, an overweaning sadness, a melancholic lassitude. And then she had spotted the first blood. After that it was a battery of ever more morbid tests, preceded by hideous fasts that left her feeling as if she were half-gone already.

And after that, it was fighting. They said from the first that she would live, that the chemo would work if the surgery didn't, that she was very lucky indeed.

As soon as she was out of the hospital, she went to the best, the most expensive restaurants, ate course after course, ate garlic and basil and drank red wine. She had bought her house, a cottage really, during the chemo, decorated it, begun putting in the garden as soon as they said she could exercise.

The world (or that tiny part of it that had heard of her) knew nothing of this. It wasn't who she was. She was neither ill nor mournful. She was Morgan Ellender the Earth Poet. That was the way she'd been described when her second volume, *Songs of Earth*, had been published—her favorite way.

The "Songs" part was an obvious homage to earlier poets, the earth part not really her idea. She had wanted to call it *Songs of Dirt*, to show that all of life, all on earth should be sung, that she embraced even the grit, even the dirt, and invited her readers to do so with her. But her friend Harmony had said there was something housewifey about it, something that suggested jingles for detergent commercials, and her publisher had agreed.

Morgan had a good publisher and good sales, for a poet. She was no Rod McKuen, indeed considered herself literary and was so considered by the literary world, but she had achieved a readership rare among her fellows. She thought it because she had something to say, something people needed in these sterile times. One interview had been headlined, "Ellender Says 'Yes!' to Life", and that pleased her.

Her poems were sensual, often erotic, heavily mythological, celebrating universal rhythms, yet frequently gritty, also celebrating the "dirt" if people wanted to call it that. She had written often of menstruation, depression, the fluids of sex, the literal dirt of the garden, the insects it harbored. And then she had rejected it all.

In those months after her marriage broke up, when she had had to leave her stepchildren as well as their father, she had wrapped herself in blankets, both literal and figurative, missing the warmth, able to do nothing but mourn. But now her hair was long, her house full of bright chintzes, and she was starting to write again, stronger poems than ever. Sexual energy flowed within her.

And this handsome stranger, Dennis Hargett, was sending out strong signals. Her last husband was a carpenter, a literate one, but a man of the earth who worked with his hands; the one before him had been a performance artist. She couldn't remember the last time she'd been out with a man in a suit. Dennis worked in television, a special projects producer. To her surprise, she liked that, she welcomed his solidity.

Harmony dragged her off to meet someone else, and that would have been the end of it if they hadn't run into each other at another party.

But she started a new poem that night, the night she met him. Images of moths came to her, moths lighting on magnolias, camellias, lilies—oddly formal flowers, all white, that seemed to need the moths, that needed their animal warmth. She had caught moths as a child and she knew they were warm in one's hand, that even these feathery, delicate things throbbed with life. She called the poem "Transfer," though she had no idea what it meant. The moths, of course, had come to the flowers; perhaps each needed something from the other. Perhaps that was the meaning. It would unfold, like wings, like petals; that was the nature of a poem.

When they met again it was only a week later and he was fresh in her mind. She had thought of him several times, had an idea well up in her, would have phoned if she'd known where he worked. (He had told her, she thought, but she was no good with number names—Channel 4, Channel 7, what was the difference?)

Seeing him again, she told him her idea, which she called Underground Aesthetics, a series on the new crop of performance artists, poets, musicians, painters who hadn't yet been noticed, but who formed a very real movement in San Francisco's cultural life. She felt a strong kinship with them, was a part of the movement herself, but she was more successful than most and slightly guilty about it.

He seemed intrigued. He said he'd phone.

When he did, she hated his voice. She hadn't realized it was so flat, so distant, so distancing, had a slightly hostile edge. It must happen when he's nervous, she thought.

They had dinner "to talk about the project", she invited

him in afterward. He took her wine glass from her hand and kissed her in earnest mid-sentence, nearly making her giggle at what she and her friends called White Man's Syndrome. (Her black friend Danielle had once lamented to a group of white women that white men obviously didn't respect her, the way they suddenly jumped her out of the clear blue. It was ten minutes before Morgan, Harmony, and company could stop laughing long enough to reassure her the behavior might be deplorable but at least it wasn't selective.)

Dennis, a big man, had been almost too insistent for comfort, but eventually Morgan had hustled him out.

It was an odd encounter, surprising, curiously . . . what? Flat? Passionless? On his part or hers? She searched for words, wanted them desperately, got out her notebook. She found her notes for "Transfer" and for the first time that evening felt comfortable. It wasn't words she needed, it was images. Why could she not remember that?

The flowers were rocks now, or salt flats, white and desolate. Tiny animals scurried there, rodents perhaps . . . prairie dogs? Prairie dogs were cheerful beasts, canine-seeming rodents, as eager to please as cocker spaniels. She fell asleep feeling better.

They had dinner again, and he told her about his current project, "Rumors and Gossip", a local game show he was developing. It was their second date—low-key, yet with undertones, memories of earlier kisses, a new one at the end. And in her dreams, the poem: Ants walking on crystals, quartz crystals, hard, mystical, the ants carrying things—bits of smaller insects.

After that, Morgan had gone away for a week, saying she'd phone when she returned. "Not at the office," he said, and gave her his home number.

14

When she returned, he had Underground Aesthetics underway and they celebrated by making love. He had specifically invited her to his condo, and she knew that was what he intended, but it almost didn't come off.

It was still daylight when they arrived, but dark in the tiny condo. It was dusty there, furnished with utilitarian simplicity. Not a picture on the walls. As she walked in, as the dark hit her, a wave of depression engulfed her. *Does he really live here?* And then: *Do I want to get involved with the person who does?* It got worse when he couldn't, in his little-used kitchen, find glasses for the margaritas he was making, and then when he did, they looked as if they hadn't been washed in a year.

But she knew something by now—she was violently attracted to him, felt irretrievably enmeshed in some unlikely but inevitable joining.

He said he too was divorced, hadn't dated in a year and a half.

"Why?" she asked.

"My standards are high."

The answer was meant to flatter, but there was something joyless in it.

"You're so alive, Morgan. I'm so attracted to you I don't know what to make of it. What do you think it's about?"

She thought she knew, and her heart sank. But the worst of it was, she felt the same. She should wait, she should get to know him better, this was dangerous . . .

The phone rang at a crucial point. The machine answered, a woman's voice said, "Dennis, this is Cathy Eicholz. We've got to talk about Rumors and Gossip; this is grossly unfair to me. I worked on that project for two years and you're not going to get away with this . . ."

Bitch! How dare she interrupt their lovemaking? What a

nasty, nasal, raspy voice she had! How furious she sounded. How did Dennis come to know such a person?

He kicked the phone off the hook.

But it was a harbinger; theirs was always a bumpy acquaintanceship. Sex was fantastic. Everything else was a little off.

A week or so into it, he called and asked if she'd like to "get together for coffee or something."

Why doesn't he just do it over the phone? She thought, sure he intended to dump her, knowing coffee was either a first date or a last. She was speechless, not wanting to go through the bother of breaking up with someone she hardly knew, but he said, "Or we could have dinner."

She had a small emergency, couldn't avoid being late, and knowing he'd come straight from work, cursed his prohibition on calling him there, a hard-and-fast rule he'd reiterated since the first time.

"Why?" she'd asked.

"I don't take personal calls at the office. Never. I just don't do it."

He was almost ebullient at dinner, as if he'd tapped into some new energy source, some secret stash.

He toasted her. "To Morgan Ellender, the world's sexiest poet." And then he said, "I have to apologize for something —when we do the series, I can't use you in the poetry section. I'm afraid it might tip our hand, as it were."

"You mean somebody might think we're dating?"

"You have to understand, I'm a very private person. I feel bad about the series, though, because that was why I sought you out; ever since I got the idea, I'd intended to use you." He shrugged. "I'm sorry it worked out this way."

"Listen, it's no problem. I wasn't looking for publicity when I suggested it—I just thought there were some really fine artists who weren't being recognized."

"What do you mean when you suggested it?"

"When I gave you the idea."

"You didn't give me the idea. You sound like this other woman who claims she thought of Rumors and Gossip."

"Don't you remember the second time we met—at Deborah Percy's party? I told you about the movement and gave you all the artists' names."

"Did you?"

They drank too much and he confessed he hated his job, had wanted something wildly different. He had wanted to be a journalist and had failed.

It was an odd confession, she thought. How many failed journalists could there be in the world? When she thought of all the unpublished poets, unnoticed painters, unloved musicians, journalism seemed a peculiar art to pine for. But she understood that this was his love, as poetry was hers, and it had been taken away; he had chosen to barter himself to a corporation, to spend his days making money, just getting through. "Sometimes I say to myself, you can do it, Dennis. Just put one foot after another. Just go in there and stay all day. And I do and next thing you know it's five o'clock."

"And then what do you do?"

"I'm with you right now."

"Yes, but when I'm not with you, I write poetry. I visit friends. I take my stepchildren to the movies. What do you do? You don't cook at home, I've seen your kitchen. Do you eat at all? Do you watch prime-time TV in a mindless stupor?"

He stared at his plate. "I don't know. How's the fish?"

Taking the hint, she changed the subject, asked about the project. He shrugged. "It's okay. It's fine. Except that most of this avant-garde stuff's pretty pathetic."

"You're not enjoying it?"

"Let's put it this way. It's not the best stuff being done."

"What isn't—the music or the painting? What *do* you like?"

"I don't know."

She learned to avoid two subjects—who Dennis Hargett might be and whether there was anything in the world he approved of or liked. Thus freed, Dennis could be witty and charming, excellent company. Their dates formed a pattern: when she was with him, she felt excited, as if they danced on a precipice, and felt empty the next day.

The first weekend he already had plans, the second he said his parents were in town, and the third it was something else. They had been "dating" if you could call it that, for nearly a month, had had sex a lot, when she mentioned to Harmony that she'd never seen him on a weekend. "Another woman," said Harmony, and she remembered his adamant order not to phone him at the office.

"I'm a very private person," he had said repeatedly now, and she could see that it was true. He never mentioned friends, much less introduced her to any. There were no photographs in his apartment, either framed or lying in casual stacks. She never saw letters there, waiting to be opened or mailed. It was the perfect set-up for a workaholic, except for one thing—he hated his work.

He was calling her less and less, exactly as someone would who was trying to stabilize an illicit affair. But somehow she didn't think it was that. What she thought was, a cold wind was blowing and she had to get out of the draft.

She phoned, her speech all planned: "Listen, I can take a hint. Really. No problem. Bye now."

But he was delighted to hear from her, chattered brightly for twenty minutes or so and asked her to a movie that week.

Had she misread the thing? Was he just out of it? She still

didn't know why he'd asked her to coffee that time—didn't he know the simplest social rituals?

"That would be nice," she said, "but you know, I feel really bad that I never get to see you on weekends. And it seems so odd I can't call you at work . . ."

His voice turned hard and flat. "Well, I'm going to retain my preference on that. But you can see me on the weekend."

"Retain your preference, will you? You sound like a legal document."

"Sorry." And he truly sounded sorry, as if he'd just gotten carried away.

"What weekend?"

"This one. Saturday."

Saturday morning the sun streamed into her cottage, revealing the dust on her coffee table, but also catching a plain glass vase full of irises and turning it into a crystal prism. Morgan took her tea into her tiny city back yard and walked around it, feeling herself its queen, examining each new flower and each bud. There were new bugs too and she welcomed them as well.

But for the first time in her garden, she felt uneasy. She found herself wanting to stay in that night, to cook, to warm herself up. She looked through cookbooks, planned a menu, went shopping. She bought Dennis a small gift, a book she knew he wanted. By mid-afternoon she had shaken the odd melancholy and settled into a contented lassitude. She talked on the phone to Harmony, washed her hair, selected music for the evening, listened to some. It wasn't a day to write, it was a day to live.

When Dennis phoned, she was bubbling. "I thought it might be nice to stay in tonight if you don't mind. I have this terrific recipe . . ."

"I had a really late lunch. I'm going to pass on that."

19

She felt the chill again, a cloud passing over the sun. He didn't seem to notice she hadn't spoken. "Look, I feel sort of—I don't want to say tired—well, yes, why don't we call it tired. I'd rather not do anything if that wouldn't anger you unduly."

She saw her hands turn blue, felt her teeth start to chatter. No such thing was happening, but the image was so strong that for a moment she was convinced of it, thrown off her stride, able to answer not as herself, Morgan, a grown woman, but only politely, like some teen-age patsy.

Harmony was a psychotherapist by trade, but declined to ply such trade unless she was getting paid for it. On this one, she laughed her head off: "This is no simple wife or neurosis problem, baby. A couple of weeks ago I thought probably mob, but now I can see it's a lot worse than that. A lot worse. There are organizations in this country that some men aren't free to talk about, you know what I mean? When our national security is at stake, it behooves us all not to ask too many questions and I know you'll want to do your part and bite that little old bullet like a good American."

Shamed, Morgan had called him back. Afterward, she never knew how she had persuaded him to come over, but thought it must have been not with words, but the icy fury in her voice. He arrived fresh-shaven, wearing knife-creased slacks and perfectly pressed button-down collar. She realized with a pang that she'd never seen him in jeans and T-shirt.

He was chattering, trying for casualness. "Should I have brought my boxing gloves?"

She handed him some wine. "This isn't about fighting."

"But you're mad."

"Mad about your breaking the date. The other stuff is more . . . well, I have my feelings hurt, that's all. The stuff like never seeing you on weekends, I mean, never being introduced to your friends . . ." She outlined it for him, the way he'd been treating the thing like a back-street liaison. "I thought when you broke the date tonight, 'oh, great, the girl friend found out and that was that.' " But it was bait, she didn't really believe it.

He said: "There is no girl friend." *Certainly not you* was as clear as if he'd said the words.

"You know we've never even rented a movie and sent out for a pizza?"

He didn't answer.

"What I'm trying to say is that the friendship element never kicked in . . . this thing has just never developed into a normal dating relationship."

He sat up straight, going off the defensive, sure of his ground. "I don't do relationships."

Had he really said that? She repeated it: "You don't do relationships."

"I told you that."

She could see her breath. "No. You didn't."

"I told you I hadn't had a date in a year and a half."

"Dennis, I work with words. That's very different from 'don't do relationships.' "

"This is what happens when you try to do somebody a favor. I wish I'd never thought of that damned 'Underground Aesthetics.' Nothing but a bunch of no-talent losers and look where it got me!"

Shocked that he'd now twice claimed his idea as her own (never mind that he was being such a baby), she couldn't let it go by: "You didn't think of it. I did."

He looked surprised. "You did?" He let a beat pass. "You know why I don't do relationships? So I won't have to have conversations like this."

"What's so bad about this?" *Compared to being treated*

like a cheap lay, for instance?

"I could have just stiffed you completely. I didn't have to come over here today."

"Well, thank you. Thank you very much for all the truly terrible things you could have done and didn't. I'm just beginning to see how grateful I ought to be."

"I didn't know anything was wrong."

"Well, no. The only way to find out would have been to have a conversation like this. And you don't have those because you don't do relationships. So you won't have to have conversations like this. So how could you know anything was wrong? But guess what? We're having one now. Read my lips: something's wrong."

"You know, you really should get to know people better before you sleep with them."

"Oh, great. If you were a rapist, you'd probably say the woman asked for it."

Red spots appeared on his cheeks. "I didn't rape you."

"Take it easy. I didn't say you did."

"I had a good time with you . . ."

"Why not? You had everything your way."

"That's another reason I don't do relationships. Everything is always on someone else's terms."

Why don't they do something about the immigration laws? Every day you see more and more of them—Martians, trying to pass.

But she knew that was a defense. As she had earlier seen her hands blue on the phone, now she saw him backed up against a wall, hanging onto the rough plaster with his fingernails, a shadow, a hundred pounds thinner, a wreck.

She felt horribly sad for him, but frightened—if you touch a corpse, its skin will rub off, it will come off on your fingers.

Could she tell him about the chill he emanated without

hurting him? No, of course not. He had treated her like a sweetie-on-the-side and she had hurt him just by calling his game. She had hurt him by asking to see him tonight, would have hurt him by presenting the paperback she'd bought him, and was now hurting him with every word she said. For him, everything hurt. Giving hurt, receiving hurt. Any time a feeling got activated, it hurt.

The words *pleasure anorexic* came to Morgan and with them a plan for a cycle of poems, a very sad cycle, the other side of her celebration of life. Like *Songs of Innocence, Songs of Experience*, she thought. *Songs of Earth, Songs of . . .* what? *Hell?* Hell was too exciting. Limbo, maybe. It would be about living life on hold. Not even living; existing in a void.

A serene look settled over his features, as it had when he'd announced that he didn't do relationships. He was once more in command. "Well, look. We were going to have to talk eventually . . ."

So it's okay to talk if you initiate it. And suddenly she saw why he hated "conversations like this"—because for once he wasn't in control. It frightened her to realize how completely she'd let him dominate.

"Now's the time, I think, to change things around a little. Why don't we just move into a friendship?"

"Dennis, you've never even mentioned friends. Do you really have any?"

"I know people. I don't know what you mean by friendship."

"Well. I don't think we can have one then."

"I thought we had a lot in common."

Did you, you superior shit who's never read a single one of my poems and never written a fucking word of your own and has the gall to call my friends no-talent losers? Is that so, you Benedict Arnold who's just committed high treason on my person? How dare

23

you, you Martian who wouldn't know a human feeling if it jumped out of your chest and rammed itself down your supercilious throat?

"Sex just muddies the waters," he said.

She breathed deeply, trying to calm herself. "Mud. That's dirt. That's earth. I could use that. I could write about that."

"You don't want to be friends?"

If he said it again, he was dead meat. She tried to summon a facsimile of his telephone voice, the one she hated so much. "I want you to go."

"Oh. Well, look,"—his tone was placating—"I really have to thank you for getting me out of my isolation . . ."

"Which made it possible for you to sexually exploit me. Excuse me if I don't say you're welcome."

"I guess I'd better go."

"I guess so."

She and Harmony got two movies, two pizzas, and lots of red wine. For awhile Harmony's husband Doug joined them, and Danielle, but finally it was just Morgan and Harmony and Dennis Quaid, to whom Harmony kept referring as "the good Dennis."

Enjoying the warmth and energy of her friends, seeing their horror as she told her story, Morgan felt the anger that had begun with Dennis's empty offer of "friendship" come to flower. It was a foul-smelling, malevolent blossom, like that of the vegetable carnivores that grow in deep, loamy woods—ugly, but it would wither and die in a day or two, and it was better than the cold, the ice he left in her vitals.

She and Harmony got silly, plotting revenge.

"Call him at the office," said Harmony, and suddenly the pitcher plant was gone, replaced by an imp.

"Yeah." Morgan was delighted. "I could wait till lunchtime, when his secretary's bound to answer the phone."

She had a great idea for a message, but Harmony said no. "Make it something intimate. Bet he hates the 'i' word. How about this: 'Tell him we got our favorite cottage at the Elk Cove Inn. I can't wait till Friday.' "

"His secretary'd probably be so thrilled for him she'd read it aloud instead of leaving it on his desk."

"He'd die."

He had died. And Morgan had left a message—not the one Harmony suggested, but the one she had first thought of. Harmony said it was no good because no one would really leave one like that, but Morgan felt the point was not belief, more a public thumbing of her nose.

The message was silly. What counted was her art. Once again she pulled out her notes for "Transfer," hoping to weave the images together and the word "weave" made her scalp prickle, turned her mind turned toward the web in which she'd been caught.

This time the image was sharp as a sting, and she drew in her breath, seeing it so stark, so vivid—the thing she hated most, feared most, the thing that had haunted her dreams when she was ill. The flowers of the first effort, of that innocent other time, were now an ice floe, a white expanse the size of a continent and on it crawled a spider. No small spider, but a spider like a tea cup, big enough to show in perfect detail against the ice. A black one. A hairy one. A long, nasty, fatbellied one, full of things it had killed.

Morgan wrote of snakes, she wrote of beetles, she nattered on about rotting wood and lichens. But deep in her heart she knew that she did not embrace everything the Earth had to offer. She did not and would not write of anything with eight legs and mandibles. She'd been told as a child that they'd kill

you—not could but would—the tiniest nip and it was cur-
tains. She'd been in a basement at the time; they were every-
where.

She wouldn't write the poem. Couldn't describe the thing,
had to get it out of her head.

The nice officers said they were Jane Patterson and Ward
Donaldson. Patterson said, "You didn't leave your last name,
is that correct? The secretary said you said he'd know. What
did you say exactly?"

"Obviously you know. You have the message slip."

"We'd like to hear it from you."

What had seemed so childishly amusing, so deliciously
silly only a few hours ago looked suddenly psychotic. Or was
Harmony right? Was it really something you couldn't take seriously?

Morgan sighed. "I guess I'd better call my lawyer." Harmony's husband Doug. Doug was a criminal lawyer,
someone used to drug dealers and white collar sleazebags. If
she'd expected him to laugh, she was mistaken.

"I'll be right over," he said. "Don't say a word."

The message she'd left for Dennis was this: "The herpes
test was positive. You'll be hearing from my lawyer."

At the time, she hadn't thought of Doug as her lawyer,
hadn't ever thought she'd need him.

As soon as she got back from the phone, mentioning
Doug's name (which they obviously recognized) and saying
he was on his way, Patterson and Donaldson started back-
pedaling.

"Ms. Ellender, I've been a fan of yours for years,"
Patterson said. "You're not a suspect in this. You're not even
the only one who ever left Hargett a message like that,
although the last one was years ago, his secretary says. If he

26

really didn't want women to call him at the office, he probably shouldn't have told them that. It's like when somebody says 'whatever you do, don't open that door.' Of course that's the door you're going to open."

She spread her hands, palms up. "We just came to you because we're trying to get some insight into this man. We've been through his calendar, his address book, his phone tape and his private correspondence if you want to call it that. His mother sent him cards on holidays, that's about it. Frankly, the guy just doesn't seem to know anybody."

"But he's a producer."

"He has a ton of professional acquaintances, but nobody who says they knew him well." She flicked something from her skirt. "Did you?"

"Know him well?"

"Yes."

"Doug said I really shouldn't talk to you."

Donaldson made a sound somewhere between a sigh and a snort. "You know there's one guy says he worked with the man for seven years, doesn't even know whether he was gay or straight."

"You dated him, that's obvious," Patterson said. "Don't you care that he's dead?"

"Of course."

But something tugged at her, a conscience-like something, telling her to level with herself, if not with these two. And looking into herself, she really couldn't summon any deep reserves of sorrow, had felt more when she had heard Elvis was dead, or Sammy Davis Jr.—men who exuded life energy. Dennis dead didn't seem that different from Dennis alive.

"Isn't there anything you can add that might help us? He just doesn't seem the sort of man anyone would bother to kill." Patterson paused, taking a breath. "I mean he didn't arouse that much emotion in people—a phone message to get his goat, that was about it."

"I found him very distant," said Morgan primly.

Doug arrived then, and the officers said they were just leaving. Nonetheless he huffed and puffed at them, and then, when they were gone, huffed at Morgan as well (about the phone message). Then he asked if she were really all right, offered to send Harmony over, kissed her, and went off to save a drug dealer.

Teapot in hand, Morgan went outside to sit in her garden. Her trumpetvine was in full flower and a joy to contemplate. But her mood was far from contemplative. Her pulse raced with the excitement of the new experience she was having— that of defying authority, keeping a secret. She had never had secret knowledge before, and it occurred to her that Dennis Hargett had lived his life as if *it* were secret knowledge. The random facts of trivia and mundaneness for which other people cared so little they broadcast, Dennis had hoarded as if they were Kruggerrands.

It would be something of an homage to him to hoard her own secret knowledge, something he would almost certainly have done if she were the one who was dead.

Morgan had a pretty good idea who had killed him and why.

The police would have known too if Dennis hadn't been so damn secretive—he had certainly erased the telltale phone message or Patterson and Donaldson wouldn't have bothered with so small a fish as Morgan.

She put herself in Cathy Eicholz's position. If she'd really cared about her show idea, if she'd worked on the idea for years as Cathy claimed she had, if perhaps she'd hoped for a job working on the show, she would have been furious, felt horribly betrayed and cheated to see Dennis claim it, time after time, as his own. He didn't, Morgan supposed, "mean any harm", as people said, he was simply too far turned inward to notice other people; they existed so dimly for him it was probably hard to imagine they could have ideas, which *were* real to him.

It was Patterson's remark about Dennis's failure to arouse emotion that had tipped Morgan off. She'd remembered Cathy's message then. It was full of emotion; red rage. Murderous rage, perhaps.

Morgan herself had never in her life done anything so stupid as leaving the phone message for Dennis. But it had seemed important. She'd felt so discounted she just wanted him to notice that she, Morgan, could have an impact on his life. What if you multiplied that feeling by a thousand or so?

Morgan watched a butterfly, sorry its life would be so short, glad hers had been given back to her. She decided definitely not to mention Cathy to Patterson and Donaldson. After all, she was a poet. While she felt she would like to steer clear of the obvious phrase regarding justice, she did see a nice irony in the situation.

Besides, Cathy was probably a person with a family and friends, people who cared about her. No one had cared about Dennis.

She took a sip of tea and leaned back, at peace. But out of the corner of her eye she caught movement. The wind was blowing white cosmos. Was it that? No, something else, something inside a flower: a spider with a moth, a moth it had caught and was wrapping somehow with strands of silk. She watched unflinching, fascinated, not even surprised she was doing so. The first line of the poem formed in her head.

Grief Counselor

I started to give Sidney Castille my usual rappity-rap. "This is Jack Beatts," I said, "with the Grief Protection Unit of the county coroner's office . . ."

That was as far as I got before he hung up.

Sidney's wife, Dawn, had died two days before in a freak accident. He'd found her with a broken neck and her copy of *Vince Mattrone's 30-day Yoga Actualizing Plan* lying on the floor beside her. It was open to the section on headstands.

I'd called him because it was my job. After the death certificates are signed, they're sent to me or one of the other grief counsellors so we can get in touch with the victim's families.

As soon as Sidney hung up, I knew he was out of touch with his feelings. He was in the first phase of the grief cycle— what we psychologists call the stage of "disbelief and denial." He was refusing to deal with death.

That's normal and that's okay, but I wanted Sidney to know he had alternatives. I had things I could share with him. So I decided to pay him a visit.

I meditated a few minutes to get myself centered and then I drove my Volkswagen over to Sidney's house on Bay Laurel Lane. It was a typical northern California redwood house set back from the road in a grove of eucalyptus. Smoke was coming out of the chimney.

As I got closer, I could see the living room through sliding glass doors that opened onto a deck. Several cats prowled in the room like tigers in a forest. Dozens of plants hung from the ceiling and took up most of the floor space as well. There was nothing to sit on but oversized cushions.

On the far wall of the room was a fireplace with a pile of books in front of it. A man was squatting there, burning the books, feeding them one by one into the fireplace.

"Sidney?" I said. "I'm Jack Beatts from . . ."

"Oh, yes, the man from the coroner's office."

He let me in and waved me to a cushion, but he didn't seem pleased about it. In fact, he went right back to feeding the fire.

"Sidney," I said, "I'm going to be up front with you. When you hung up, I sensed I'd better get over here right away."

"Yeah, that's what I thought. I guess I panicked when you said 'coroner's office.' "

"A lot of people are uptight about that. But I'm going to ask you to forget about the bureaucracy and just be open with me."

"I guess we may as well get it over with." He put a copy of *Zen Flesh, Zen Bones* in the fireplace and turned around to face me. A tear rolled down each cheek.

"That's it, Sidney," I said. "Flow with it. Experience your feelings."

"You talk like Dawn."

"I know how it is, Sidney. Everything reminds you of her, doesn't it? But that's okay at this stage. I don't want you to be negative about it."

"*Negative!*" he snorted. "What am I supposed to . . ."

"I'll bet those are Dawn's books you're burning." He nodded. "And it looks like you're about to take the cats to the pound. You're getting rid of everything that reminds you of Dawn, aren't you?"

Tears came into his eyes again. "I couldn't take it any more,

31

Mr. Beatts. I never should have married her in the first place."

"I know where you're coming from, Sidney. You felt inadequate because you were a lot older than Dawn, right?"

"She was twenty-two," he said, "and looking for a Daddy. A rich daddy. And I was just lonely, I guess. I picker her up hitchhiking on my way out here from Ohio after my first wife died." He winced. "But *she* died of natural causes."

"Death *is* natural, Sidney. I mean life is a circle, you know? I want you to choose to recognize that. And if burning books is what's happening for you, I don't want you to feel guilty about it. Just acknowledge that it's okay."

"Look, are you going to take me in or what?"

"Take you in? Oh, you mean to the Grief Center."

"Is *that* what they call it in California?"

"For sure. We can rap anywhere you like if the vibes are wrong here."

"What is a vibe, Mr. Beatts? If I heard Dawn use that word once I . . ."

"Now stay loose, Sidney. I hear what you're saying and I sense you're uptight about it. You couldn't relate to Dawn's lifestyle, right?"

He began picking up cats and taking them to the carriers on the deck. I didn't want to blow the energy we had going, so I followed along beside him.

"She was all caught up in what they call the human potential movement," he said. "Transactional analysis, transcendental meditation, self-actualization, bioenergetics, biofeedback . . ."

"She must have been a heavy lady."

"She talked funny. Like you. And she cooked things like wheat germ soufflé. And she wanted the house to be 'natural.' You couldn't go to sleep without a cat curled around your neck, or a spider plant tickling your nose. It got so every time

I saw her do that crazy yogurt . . ."

"Yoga."

He closed the last carrier and we went back into the house.

"I used to call it yogurt to annoy her," he said, squatting by the books again. "Anyway, when she started to stand on her head, she'd do it first with her feet against the wall and then she'd let go of the wall and stick her legs up in the air. Well, every time I saw her with her feet like that, getting little toeprints all over the paint, I'd think how easy it would be just to grab her and . . ." He stopped.

"And what?"

"And snap her neck."

I nearly clapped him on the back I was so relieved. At last he'd gotten his energy flowing in a positive way! "I have to acknowledge you, Sidney," I said. "It's really a far out thing to see someone being so open about his fantasies."

Sidney tried to speak, but he couldn't. He took out a handkerchief and blew his nose. Sometimes you have to hurt people to help them so I took a chance.

"You killed her, didn't you, Sidney?" I said.

He kept his eyes down as he put the handkerchief back in his pocket. "You knew all along," he said finally.

"For sure," I said supportively. "Self-recrimination is very common in the first stage of the grief cycle, and I want you to know that it's okay."

"Okay?" he said. "I don't understand."

"A lot of people get on that kind of trip when something like this happens. You and Dawn weren't getting along and you feel guilty about it now, right? You think she died because of something in your karma."

The way Sidney looked at me I could tell he was surprised. He didn't really expect anyone else to understand. He started to speak, but I stopped him.

"That's okay," I said. "You know? Because it's only the first part of the cycle. You know what's next? Personality reorganization! Sidney, you've got a really positive thing to look forward to."

Sidney sat down on one of the cushions and started to laugh. It doesn't happen often that somebody really flashes on the whole cycle like that, and it was a far out thing to see.

"Mr. Beatts," he said. "I don't remotely understand where you're coming from . . ."

"Don't try, man."

"But I think I can flow with it."

Where the Boys Are

One day, kaboom—forty-seven, overweight, graying, divorced, devastated. What to do?

No problem for little me. Being a red-blooded American girl, perhaps ever-so-slightly influenced by the surrounding culture and media, I knew the cure for each of those conditions.

I had a chemical peel, dropped fifteen pounds, got my hair frosted, enjoyed a fling with a younger man, and started drinking too much.

The first three were keepers, but I got sick of babysitting the boy toy and nursing the hangovers.

Next.

Well, next I went back to Diet Coke and long nights with old movies. And then I got my real estate license and asked my friends to fix me up with nice, solid men my own age. How did I know they'd laugh in my face?

By now, two years had passed and I'd remade myself. I even more or less understood what made Jerry dump me—he'd grown and I hadn't. I was dumpy and boring. I had no life besides him and the kids—and once the kids were grown I must have seemed like a barnacle. (Of course there's nothing so clingy as a girl under thirty, but in Tiffany's case, he must think it's a good thing.)

Anyway, now I had a profession, a good figure, and a great haircut. What I needed was some witty conversation and someone to go to parties with.

Well, actually that's a big fat lie.

I know it, you know it, and my mother knew it the second I told it. What I needed was true and abiding love. Why should I be different from all other women?

My mom said, "Shana, remember the movie? You go where the boys are, that's all."

"Mom, that wasn't about dating. It was about spring break."

"So give yourself a spring break. Go where the boys are."

"You mean football games? Investment seminars? Give *me* a break."

"What's so wrong with that?"

"I want a guy who's interested in the things I am."

"Like what?"

"Like ballet. I need someone to take me to the ballet."

"Ha! You need a girl friend."

Nonetheless, she set me thinking. I did the next thing the culture says to do, after losing weight and turning your hair half a dozen colors. I made a list of the qualities I wanted in a man and then I narrowed it down.

There were only four things he absolutely had to have: intelligence, wit, compassion, and some kind of success. He didn't have to be president of a company, but I wasn't up for picking up restaurant tabs.

Curiously enough, it wasn't my mother, it was my friend Amy who said, "Doesn't he have to be Jewish?"

That had been on the original list, but I could live without it.

"The JCC has singles nights," she said.

The Jewish Community Center. It was a thought. If it had come from my mother, it wouldn't have been remotely acceptable, but Amy was hip. Hip, but married—meaning she hadn't checked out singles night, but swore she would in my shoes.

So I did.

And what do you know, it was pretty hip, and there was this sort of halfway presentable guy there. About six-three, good shoulders, nice smile.

Well, actually, the guy was adorable if you like the confident type. Butch, his name was. Butch Wagner.

He was about my age, I thought, and he was lean, as if he did a lot of running. I was pretty sure he was sneaking looks at me during the little talk that served as the excuse for the gathering (singles have to do *something* together and on this occasion it was listen to a lecture on vacation swaps).

It was a good topic—it could stimulate discussion on where someone likes to go, what she likes to do, whether or not she'd ever consider camping (I for one, probably would, which couldn't have been said two years ago.) Anyway, you could kind of get an idea from the question and answer period who was a complete jerk and who wasn't. But it was academic. There was really only one cute guy of a certain age.

We'd both been to Russia and loved it—how many people can say that? Instant bonding.

Or a start, anyway. We went for coffee—the universal first date—and ended up giggling so much we moved up to dinner on our second.

Butch certainly met the criteria. He was a financial counselor by trade, and better yet, an acquaintance of mine knew him. He'd moved to town a few months ago, newly divorced, and invited my friend and her husband to his summer home in Connecticut. So he had community standing and demonstrable bucks.

He had intelligence and wit, no question—could keep me laughing for hours. Compassion certainly; he couldn't have been nicer to Mitzi, my poor old blind dog.

And he was sexy; he was even Jewish. He played tennis, he liked Russia. Oh, God, I was falling in love.

It happened fast for both of us. Pretty soon we were together every night, one night his place, the next night mine, always doing something fun, something different—even, believe it or not, attending the ballet.

After a month or so, he gave me a necklace made of silver beads, each one different, probably from India. A just-right gift—it said he cared, but wasn't so expensive it seemed like a bribe. But then, he was a just-right kind of guy—for me. That was the point. He was just perfect for me.

What I liked, he liked; what I thought, he agreed with. I never thought to notice that I was always the first to express an opinion; he the one who was quick to chime in. (Surely you don't think the ballet was his idea.)

It was so intense; it happened so fast. Love, love, love—ah, to find it at last; at my age, after so much misery. Those were heady days—and I could tell he felt the same.

The big moment arrived with fanfare. First he sent me a hat—a beautiful hat that arrived from Saks. Then he invited me for lunch at Arnaud's, and after that announced I had a ten a.m. appointment to get my hair done. When I got to the salon, it turned out I was also signed up for a manicure and pedicure, also prepaid. He sure knew how to pamper.

He'd made it into the grandest of occasions. He'd be showing up with a ring box, not a doubt in my mind.

But, alas, he didn't show at all. Or at least he didn't for twenty minutes. I was just beginning to worry when my purse sang out, causing frowns from nearby diners. My cell phone. I jerked it out. "Butch?" My voice was ragged.

"Shana, I could shoot myself." He lowered his voice. "Mrs. Vickery's having a crisis." I knew all about Mrs. Vickery—his favorite eighty-year-old client who had more money than God and didn't need investment advice so much as she needed a friend. "Listen, I—uh—can't really talk about it right now, but it seems to be triggered by the death of an old friend. Darling, I could die, I really could, but I've got my hands full right now. Can you bear with me a little bit?"

Well, I wanted a compassionate man.

"Why don't you go ahead and order and I'll get there as soon as I can?"

I did, but I could barely nibble. I missed him far too much to even think about eating. And here I was all dolled up, fingers and toes and everything. Eating alone just wasn't on the program.

I tried him on my cell phone, but couldn't get him. It must mean he was on the way, I thought. But it didn't take more than twenty minutes to get from his office to the French Quarter, and several twenty-minute intervals passed before I finally left nearly in tears, the table a mess of crumbs from bread shredded and crushed in anxiety.

My stomach clenched and cramped as I drove home, knowing I'd never see him again, that this was his cowardly, contemptible way of getting out of a relationship that had progressed too quickly, that men were scum and I was stupid. I didn't know the half of it.

If I'd eaten anything, I'd have thrown up when I opened the door. My house was stripped.

Not stripped clean. He'd left everything worthless or even ordinary. Only the antiques were gone and the oriental rugs, all the silver, of course, all my jewelry, and a quite valuable collection of photographs that had had to be pointed out. Not that I volunteered it. I could remember it vividly: "Those are wonderful. Tell me about them."

When I thought about it, he'd wanted to know about lots of things, *including* my jewelry. Straight men aren't interested in jewelry; why hadn't that occurred to me?

Because I thought this one was special—more sensitive and aesthetically inclined than most. A perfect soulmate.

I didn't even go upstairs before I tried to call the cops, didn't even ask the neighbors if they'd seen a van or a truck pull up; I just went for the nearest phone. And found it missing. Stolen. Whereupon I burst into tears. The guy stole my phone! Talk about insult upon injury.

I never felt more like an ass than when I tried to tell the story to the nice detective, who actually wore a trenchcoat. Yes, Butch had a key. Well, sure, I'd only known him six weeks, but he—well, I couldn't say it. I certainly couldn't say he was just the kind of guy you would trust—anybody would—you just *knew*. I couldn't say I felt so close to him it was like we were already married, that we were as alike as two peas, we thought and felt so similarly we were probably made from the same DNA. And I sure wasn't going to say I'd actually given him the key after we'd first slept together, which was about a week and a half after we met.

No, I didn't know his first name—other than Butch—but that was this game we played, see, he'd try to make me guess . . .

Nobody wants to confront their own stupidity. Their demons, maybe—but not their dopiness. Oh, God, I felt a fool! At first I was so embarrassed I forgot to be sad because I'd lost my soulmate. Or mad because I'd been betrayed.

But all that came. The sad part lasted about thirty seconds and the mad part never did go away. I had plenty of time for the gamut of emotions, and there was quite an array, one delightful one being fear of what Jerry was going to think, what the neighbors were saying, even of my two kids' reactions—which I was sure would be sympathy. (Actually I was only half-right—one was sympathetic, the other contemptuous, and truth be told, I preferred the sympathy.)

The Trenchcoat Kid's name was Gary Breaux and if not for my recent tragic experience and the ring on his left hand, I might have been up for a little flirting. He was tall and built a little like a barrel, more or less blond with a lush moustache, and he had such an *earnest* air about him. Butch had had no such thing, which was probably why he was so attractive.

Breaux kept a perfectly straight face while I confessed my misplaced trust, though I know it cost him, and he went all out, calling the crime lab even though this was such a professional job there were bound to be no prints, hairs, or matchable DNA. Then he canvassed the neighbors, who had indeed seen a truck—a plain one with no logo—along with one white guy and two black ones. The white guy was the one I'd been hanging with, so naturally they didn't think anything of it—especially since I was getting divorced. Who knew? Maybe the furniture was going to go to Jerry's, maybe my kids were getting it, maybe Butch and I were moving in together and we were making room for his stuff. The heist was so public, a criminal explanation didn't occur to them.

Without fingerprints, a social security number, or even an age, there was no way of tracing Butch, especially since that undoubtedly wasn't his name. But Detective Breaux did check out the few meager facts Butch had given me about himself—grew up in St. Louis, went to Yale, that sort of thing—but of course he didn't and hadn't.

The house in Connecticut turned out to have been rented to a Bill Smith at the time my friends visited.

Breaux did find the moving company Butch had hired—the one with the plain truck and the two black employees—but the two men were casual labor whose names the company didn't have. We put out a reward on the tip line, and one of them came in—or someone who said he was did. He said they'd unloaded the furniture into a U-Haul van. By now,

Butch would have had time to drive it anywhere in the country, turn it in, and disappear again. He probably had the routine down.

After quite a bit of nagging on my part, Breaux decided that was probably right, and bestirred himself to call a couple of pals in other big departments to see if they'd ever had a similar complaint. And one of them, bless his heart, had heard of one—it seems he spent a lot of time on the Internet, where he belonged to a cop bulletin board, and he just asked his cyberpals if it rang a bell.

It did. Somebody in Dallas knew about a nearly identical case—handsome dude comes to town, meets unsuspecting woman and cleans her out. Breaux got her name and called her and got the particulars—same description, same vague lie about "investment counseling" (*how* could I have been so dumb?), same cute meet. That's right—the Jewish Community Center. Singles night.

Oh, boy. Butchie-boy didn't know it, but he had met his nemesis. Yes, indeed. Me, Shana Goldsmith, the Pantyhosed Avenger. If women stick together, think about Jewish women. Think about *aggrieved* Jewish women.

Did you know that Jews make up only 2.1 per cent of the population? There aren't that many of us, and we all have cousins and aunts and nieces. Where did he think he was going to hide?

All I had to do was start calling around—get up a phone tree, maybe.

I planned the whole thing—getting diabolical pleasure out of it—while cooking dinner for my daughter and her husband, who were hovering solicitously in the wake of the late unpleasantness. Convinced they were going to think I was a genius, I laid it out for them. They exchanged a glance and I could see distress in it: *Oh, God. She's finally flipped.*

But it wasn't that at all. Mindy said, "Mom, there's an easier way. You know what a database is?"

Oooh, I was dumb—why didn't I think of that? I said, "Sure. They're in computers."

"Well, you can access them with computers."

Phil said, "Bulletin boards too—that's better yet. Jewish conferences." He was starting to look excited. "This could work. Why don't you let us do a search for you?"

Six months ago, I would have said, "Sure." I would have been thrilled to let someone else do it. But not now. No way. I was the Pantyhosed Avenger. Nobody else.

The next day I went out, got myself a laptop, and made another meal for the kids. After dinner they taught me the basics of the Internet.

It ended up taking me two or three days to feel confident—two or three days, working ten hours a day. But after that, there was no stopping me. I joined bulletin boards right and left, quickly learning that, though Jews may comprise only about two per cent of the population, most of the two per cent appear to be travelers on the Information Highway. There were dozens of Jewish bulletin boards and tons of Jewish conferences within general ones. My work was cut out for me.

I tried different approaches. In one, I started a topic called "Singles Nights." Another was called "to Catch a Gonif." One was simply, "Red Alert" and one was "Women Beware." All bore fruit. That is, all attracted plenty of interest and lots of promises to check out the local singles night.

And guess what? People came through. Most reported nothing, but at least they did it. I was about a week into it when I got an E-mail from someone calling herself "Gladebabe" in Miami: "Just saw your post on AOL and freaked out! My sister's dating him—I'm not kidding. His name's still Butch, by the way. Margie says he's got a really weird tattoo."

Okay, now you know. I fell for a man with a mermaid on his thigh.

Breaux set up a meeting with a Sergeant Donaldson in Miami, and the two of us got together with Margie, whose younger sister had already shown her my posts on various services. Whatever tears she'd cried were now history and what Donaldson and I saw before us was one furious woman-about-to-be-scorned.

She was forty-five, maybe, and looked thirty-five, a little hefty in the hips, but slim in the thighs and light on her feet. She had blond hair—the kind that's meant to cover gray, and does, and a face that was pretty, but pretty wasn't the best thing about it. It was impish, full of fun, strong of spirit. She made jokes all the time she was describing her heartbreak and—far worse—her humiliation at having fallen for the guy.

To say I could empathize goes without saying, but I would have been crazy about her in any case. Here was a terrific woman—I was proud to be in such company.

She finished her story and turned not to Donaldson, but to me. "Okay, Nancy Drew—what now?"

But Donaldson answered. "We need to get Shana to identify him."

"Well, I'm supposed to have lunch with him tomorrow."

"Uh-oh," I said. "I hope he didn't make you a hair appointment first."

"Uh-uh. I knew you were coming, so I asked *him*. I thought we'd go to a nice al fresco kind of place. If you get my drift."

"Ah. Sidewalk dining. The sergeant and I can just stroll by."

"Better. It's in a mall. You can go to the second floor and

44

look down with binoculars."

Donaldson said, "Either of you ladies need a job? I seem to be kind of superfluous here."

So then we had to spend fifteen minutes soothing his ego.

But he came in handy the next day. He and I went up to the second floor of the mall and waited for the handsome couple, whereupon Donaldson handed me the binoculars. I made a positive ID and he was all set to go down and introduce himself, when Butch pulled something from his pocket.

"He's giving her something. Omigod, it's a necklace."

One I recognized, made out of silver beads.

I waited while Donaldson made the bust, and as Butch was getting up, Margie gave me the thumbs-up. Slowly, he turned around, in time to see me return the sign. He looked puzzled for a moment, and then I took off my hat and glasses. The look on his face was the most beautiful thing I ever hoped to see.

"Hey, Shana," Margie hollered. "I got your necklace back for you." And he looked even sicker.

Fresh Paint

Officer, would you like some coffee? I made some for the ladies and gentlemen of the press, but they too excited to have any—gettin' they pictures and all. Wonder who call the po-lice on me? Maybe it wasn't them atall. Coulda been Tomika, 'cross the way—she always did have a thing for Cleon.

Now, don't you worry 'bout Cleon; he be all right. Come on, let me get you some coffee, then we talk about it. What? You gon' let him loose now? Oh, you want me to. Uh-uh. You take the key—I'm not lettin' 'im loose. He can stay handcuffed to that bed the rest of his miserable life as far as I'm concerned. He a piece of art himself now. Got videos, got photographs; only thing I regret is you ain't gon' give me time to paint him.

Oh, yeah, 'course I already painted him. I mean, next I want to paint the bed, with him lyin' in it painted up like he is. That'd make a right good picture, don't ya think? Where's that art critic? Mr. Turkelson? Hey, Mr. Turkelson—what you think of that one? Look authentic to ya? You gon' take back what ya said in court?

'Scuse me, Officer, I got a laughing fit comin' on. Every time I look at that picture, I get a fit of the giggles. Would somebody give me a handkerchief, please? 'Scuse me, I just can't seem to stop.

All right.

All right, Officer. I know it must be hard on you, bein' the odd one out like this. But you don't need to get so upset about it. Say, you one o' those new out-o'-town recruits they gettin'? 'Cause otherwise you mighta' heard of Cleon and Orietta Banks. We famous. And he rich.

In fact—oh, me, I got another laughin' fit comin' on—in fact, if you went lookin' in your po-lice computer, you'd see Cleon famous in there, too. Oh, yeah. Car theft, strong-arm robbery, armed robbery, assault, bank robbery—least some of those. Possession of this, sale of that, burglary, shopliftin' —I know he did 'em all, just not sure which ones they got him for.

What's that? Has he done time? Ohhh, yeah. Forgive me for laughin' again, Officer. Oh, yeah, Cleon's done time. Cleon's done time big time. See, tha's part of his gig. He a outlaw. If he wasn't a outlaw, he be just another dude can't draw worth a damn, but he a outlaw. Young girls put up with that stuff.

Can't say they like it; won't say that. But Cleon and me had a baby together twenty-five years ago—I wasn't but seventeen at the time. Cleon, he was twenty-two if I remember right. I thought I was queen of the Magnolia Project. Had myself such a good-lookin' man, already grown-up and out of high school. He was doin' good too. Had a job and everything. Worked at a warehouse. He tol' me, "Ori, the folks at this place are so dumb I wouldn't lower myself to work with 'em if I didn't know what was gon' happen—they gon' make me a supervisor soon. I'm gon' do real good and I'm always gon' be there for Shawana." Shawana—that's our daughter. And you know what? He didn't lie. I mean, he didn't quite lie. He always been there for Shawana. Whenever he out of jail.

Well, in a kind of a way he has.

I b'lieve he was right, though—he probably was smarter than the folks at that warehouse. Ain't nothin' dumb about Cleon—he just like a cat. Know how to get somebody to take

47

care of him, no matter how bad he scratch up the furniture.
He probably wasn't lyin' about his future, either—probably
woulda been a supervisor, brains had anything to do with it.
But Cleon—just like he know how to get around people (spe-
cially me)—he know how to mess up. Did in those days,
anyway. Can't afford to no more—he got two convictions;
can't get another one. Mmm mmm, no sir. He ain' gon' go
back to Angola for the rest of his life—had to figure out
somethin' else.

How 'bout a doughnut to go with that coffee, Officer?
Cleon all right. He gon' sleep at least another half-hour,
maybe forty-five minutes. I know the man. I got some nice
muffins here—won't you have one? What's that? Oh, yeah,
the warehouse. Well, he worked at some place sell TVs and
things—Circuit City, Campo, some kind of thing like that. I
don't know if they didn't have guards or what. And I really
don't know how he think he could get away with it; all I know
is the rest of the way Cleon think. He think what's yours is
his, you understand me? So Cleon just take home whatever
look good to him—run a little resale business, right out of his
house.

What's that, Officer? Maybe I did say he was a little bit
smart—mostly I said he say he smart. Well, you right. He got
caught. 'Course he got caught.

Got caught, got convicted, went to jail.

He get out of jail, he start doin' drugs. Smokin' 'em,
snortin' 'em, sellin' 'em, everything. All of a sudden, Cleon
the drug king. Well, maybe he do drugs before, but never
like this. I wouldn't have nothin' to do with him. Oh, and by
this time, I got another child with him. Baby boy name
Kwayne.

What you mean, why was I still seein' him? I wasn't, then.
Got pregnant just about he time he got caught. Had the baby

while he was in jail, and wouldn't let him nowhere 'round me once he start doin' all them drugs. My mama didn't drop me from no turnip truck.

Matter of fact, I wouldn't even let him see his own baby boy. But, Cleon, he a good father. No, Officer, really. He love his babies. And he hate to see us so poor. I'm sorry to say I was on welfare at the time, and you know how welfare is. Can't hardly get off it, 'cause it's so hard to get a job that pays enough to cover ya child care. And can't make much money and keep ya benefits. So all I had at the time were little cleanin' jobs—two or three little half-day things. We havin' a hard time, Shawana and me and Kwayne.

So you know what Cleon do? I give him credit for this, give him all the credit in the world. He clean up for a while there. He get off drugs—go to some neighborhood detox place—but he always say, "Ori, I ain't no addict; just don't have the addictive personality, I can do drugs if I want, I just don't want to right now. Want to get my family back."

My family! he say. We weren't no family, Officer—at the best of times, Cleon, he come 'round once, twice a week. Tha's the kind of family it was. But this time he impress me. He clean up, he get a job, and we get married.

We had a real nice time there for awhile. Cleon, he a good father. Even go to church on Sunday. Work hard, come home at night—everything copacetic. Had some job in a hospital, didn't really mean much, but it was all right. It was just fine till he got fired.

What's that? No, it wasn't for stealing drugs. Officially, he was just laid off, but you know what it really was? Somebody's kid needed that job. Political thing, you know what I mean? Well, everything still mighta been all right if he'd'a just gone out and got another job. Which he could have. No, he didn't really have no skills, but there lots of jobs for people who show up on time—that's all you gotta do, just show up. 'Stead, he let those fool friends of his talk him into robbin' a bank.

He say he gon' get a job, he just need the money to tide us over. Well, in a way it make sense—we didn't have enough money to last till he got a pay check. Still, the landlord probably wasn't gon' throw us out just 'cause we two weeks late on the rent. 'Course it wouldn'ta been the first time, and he'd threatened and everything. But my mama woulda taken us in, maybe. Just no need to go rob a bank. No need in the world.

'Scuse me, Officer? Yeah. Sure did. Got convicted again. Went to Angola again. Two-time loser, tha's what you call that, ain't it, Officer?

'Cept this time Cleon come out a winner.

He learn a skill in prison. Well, really he kind of teach it to himself. But he had help; I'm not sayin' he didn't have help. He had a inmate friend called Blind Joey who show him a whole new way to be. Now Blind Joey couldn't see his hand in front of his face, but he could paint. I gotta stop and laugh a little here. Least, there was this New Orleans gallery thought he was the Michelangelo of the penal system.

He'd paint these little stick figure scenes, folks out in the fields, or maybe standin' around on the porch of a sto'—you ever see that kind of picture? Yeah, you right—everybody has.

Well, Blind Joey's was more innerestin' than most because he couldn't see his paints, so you never knew what color anything was gon' be, and also, he couldn't see what he already painted, so things got jumbled up a little. Yeah, go ahead and laugh. Dahveed—he the gallery owner—I'm sure he prob'ly laugh all the way to the bank. But I gotta give it to him—those ol' jumbled-up, funny-colored pictures come out pretty good. They got they own style, you know what I mean? Blind

Joey ain't paintin' no more, though—somebody stab him seven, eight years ago—jealous, I guess.

'Course Dahveed love that—couldn't be better for business. He handle what they call outsider artists. You unnerstand what that is? It's kind of self-explanatory, ain't it? Well, for outsiders, you can't hardly beat outlaws, officer. Yeah, I see you makin' that face. You think you feelin' sick now, I'm 'bout to really turn your stomach. You know some of the most famous murderers behind bars is artists now? Anybody can do it. Or mos' anybody. And it pays so good it's almost like robbin' a bank. I guess tha's one of the main things attracted Cleon—that and the fact he couldn't afford no more mess-ups.

While he and Blind Joey both at Angola, he ax Blind Joey some things, like what kind of paint to use and how to mix it up—few little things like that. And then he just dig in and paint.

What, Officer? I hear ya. I know how bad that make ya feel, out tryin' to make a livin', and this outlaw get somethin' for nothin' just 'cause he is a outlaw. No, it ain't right. I agree with you on that one.

It might not'a been right, but all the same I was overjoyed. I was the man's wife, after all. It wasn't dangerous and it was legal. Only thing was, it wasn't exactly lucrative. Somebody like Blind Joey, now, he made pots o' money. But Cleon—well, frankly, Cleon wasn't all that good. He a little too—I know this gon' sound funny, considerin' we talkin' 'bout a bank robber here, but Cleon just a little too timid. No, I'm tellin' you the truth—what it was, he didn't have the confidence of his own convictions. Or maybe he just didn't have no convictions; wouldn't be surprised. To my mind, he draw everything too little—kinda constipated lookin', scared to get up there and be what it is. Then he be stuck with a great big sky, and he fill it in with flyin' crosses, kind of like polka dots. I ax him once why he put 'em there and he say he don't know what else to put there, and people like Jesus, so he thought he'd try him some crosses. Can you credit that, Officer? That was the best answer he could come up with.

No, them crosses didn't have wings. They was more like floatin' than flyin', maybe, just kind of hangin' there in the part of the canvas that wasn't filled in.

Well, I tell him that and he say, "You think you can do better, bitch?" Just like that. Tha's the way my husband talk to me.

I jus' want to make peace in the family, so I say, "You know what I think's real good? I like that little dancin' man there."

The picture we was lookin' at was a man playin' a piano and some people dancin', only they mostly look like they got flagpoles up they butts. 'Scuse me, Officer, but how would you say it? There was this one man, though, look like he was havin' fun. So I say to Cleon, "Why don't you do just this one man? Make him real big and don't have nothin' much else in the picture."

And Cleon say, "Shut up, Ori, you don't know what you talkin' about."

So I show him. I go ahead and I paint it. I paint it kinda like he paint it and kinda different. I make the man dance crazier; crazier and wilder with his hair flyin' all around. And Cleon, he don't say nothin'. But then, next day, I get me another idea; I want to put a moon over the dancin' man's head. But I can't find the picture.

I ax him where my picture is and he say he don't know. But then I notice all of a sudden he doin' what I said. He tryin' to make all his people bigger, tryin' to fill up the canvas with 'em, really make 'em stick out. But somehow—now there

ain't nothin' wrong with this, it's just the way Cleon paint—
somehow they don't look right. It just ain't Cleon style, tha's
all. His style be makin' a whole lot of little figures, look like
they 'mos lost on the canvas.

Now, I go to church reg'lar and I can certainly open up my
heart when I know I been wrong. So I say, "Cleon, I'm real
sorry for what I said. You was right all along. I shouldn'ta
messed with what you tryin' to do. You tol' me I didn't know
what I was talkin' about and it was true."

He say, "No, Ori. No, I think you got somethin' there. I
just got to get the hang of it, tha's all. How 'bout you do me
another one, maybe another couple, so I can study 'em."

Now in all these years of marriage, I could probably count
on the fingers of one hand the number of times Cleon con-
cede me a point. I shoulda realize somethin' was fishy. But
you know what? I really did enjoy paintin' that picture—it
was somethin' I just kind of knew I could do and sure enough
I could. So when Cleon say make him a couple more, I look
forward to it. I wait till the chirren off at school and I turn on
WWOZ and I sit down to paint and I think, "Now what am I
gon' paint?" Well, they playin' a Billie Holiday song on the
radio and I think, "Yeah! I'm gon' paint Billie Holiday;
I'm gon' make her real beautiful, more than she really was,
because she deserves it, an' then I'm gon' put a gardenia in
her hair."

So I make me a midnight blue background, 'cause Billie
the blues queen, and then I paint me a great big beautiful picture of her. She wearin' a kind of wine-color dress, with red
tones in her skin, and she got a gardenia that's not really
white, but maybe kinda yellow and kind of gold in certain
places. Beautiful. Just beautiful.

The whole picture about two feet wide, maybe three feet
tall—different shape from what Cleon paint. See, he like hori-

zontal shapes—that way he can get in all them little bitty figures, and he don't have that much sky to fill in with flyin' crosses.

Well, Billie never look so good. She got everything but an audience. So, know what I did? I put in that little dancin' man—same one I made big that I kinda lost track of.

By this time, I was feelin' so pleased with myself I start to get ideas. I think, what about if I paint African-American musicians? (I was still listenin' to WWOZ.) So I thought maybe some old-timey ones—like Robert Johnson, with that ol' derby hat—and then I could do livin', breathin' ones, nothin' says I couldn't. What about if I just got out a old CD cover with a picture of Aaron Neville on it and paint Aaron himself? Hey, how 'bout Fats Domino? Ernie K-Doe? These gentlemen not gettin' any younger. Could do with some recognition, maybe. Then I really get grandiose. I think, what if I paint Fats Domino from a photograph and then maybe photograph the paintin' and send it to him? Maybe he buy it. See what happen to me, Officer? One mornin' paintin' one picture and already I got big ideas.

Fantasies, really. I didn't really b'lieve none of that—I was just havin' fun. Well, I did paint Robert Johnson and I see he need something, just like Billie. So I give him the dancin' man for a audience as well, and about then Cleon come home. I say, "What you think?" And he say, "Tha's pretty interestin', Ori. Kinda childlike, doesn't show much technique, but I b'lieve I'm gon' think on it some."

Next day, the chirren be off to school, Cleon out somewhere chewin' the fat with his friends, and I go in the garage, which Cleon use for a studio in those days. I go out there, but I don't see my pictures.

Humph, I think; that's pretty strange. But I don't really care, because I want to do Fats. So I do him, and this time I put a bit more care into it, take my time a little—yesterday I was in a big hurry because Cleon ax me to do a couple. I realize now I was afraid I wouldn't get 'em done. So I do Fats real careful—just a beautiful picture of Fats, but he don't look right without the dancin' man, so I put him in the corner. And then Cleon come home and he so happy I think he even more loaded than usual. "Orietta! Honey, we done struck gold," he say, and he come up behind me, put his arms around me and near about make me mess up my beautiful picture.

But I couldn't get mad if we struck gold, so I turn around, happy as a new bride, and I say, "What is it, Cleon, honey? You have a good day at the track?"

And he say, "Lot better than that, Miz Banks. Our ship has come sailin' right into the harbor. You know that first picture you did? The Dancin' Man? Dahveed sold it for a thousand dollars! So I took him the other two pictures and he say he can get even more for 'em—maybe twice as much, he say."

Well, I'm just starin' at him, my mouth open, my eyes big as saucers, and he say, "Orietta, we really on to somethin' here. That new paintin' style of ours gon' take me a long way. Yessir! Dahveed say I'm gon' be rich and famous—say I've just made a artistic breakthrough."

Yeah, Officer, you notice that too? I never was that good at grammar, but I know the first person singular when I hear it. So naturally I say what has to be said and Cleon get mad. He say, "Woman, don't ruin this for us! I'm the one got the name; not you. Dahveed can't say Orietta Banks paint those pictures—whoever heard of Orietta Banks? Also, you a woman. You see the problem there? You just name me a famous woman artist. Was Michelangelo a woman? Leonardo da Vinci? Go ahead. Name one."

I shoulda name Clementine Hunter, but he sneak up on me.

All I can say is, "Famous? You gon' be famous, Cleon?"

"And rich," he say.

Well, yeah, Officer, I do see what happen to my pronoun, but he had me. He tell me Dahveed don't handle no women artists, he'd laugh me right out of there if I come in and say I done those pictures. So I just shut up about it.

And you know what? Everything Cleon predicted come to pass.

Cleon got famous and we got rich. Well, yeah—you mentioned you never heard of us. Well, Officer, with all due respect, are there that many artists you can name? You know 'bout a man put a little blue dog in all his pictures? No? Well, he even more famous than Cleon—come to think of it, probably got the dog idea from us, 'cause after that I put the dancin' man in every picture I ever paint. For luck.

And oooeeee—did we have it. Everybody buy those pictures. What's that? Yep, white folks did. And black folks! Officer, I can tell you in all modesty that there is hardly any African-American celebrity who doesn't have a Cleon Banks—and there's part of the problem right there.

I'll get to that part in a minute, but right now I want you to understand the point I'm tryin' to make with you. Maybe you aren't real up on the art world, but if you went to Cleon's house in Eastover, you'd see how successful he is. I mean, you wouldn't think so from this place of mine, but now maybe you gettin' some inkling what this whole show's about.

What's that—you got a cousin in Eastover? Mighty fine neighborhood, ain't it? And I know what you thinkin'—you thinkin' once we started makin' it, my life musta been real sweet. Uh-huh. I knew you was thinkin' that.

Well, it mighta been; it coulda been. And up to a point it really was. Only problem was Cleon. The man drinks, Officer, honey.

Oh. Oh, I see. I'm sorry, Officer, I meant no disrespect. I just thought, since you a woman, too, you might understand a man who gets a snootful and then get too big for his britches. Well, now, come to think of it, I take that back. Cleon too big for his britches the minute he wake up to the minute he go to bed—or more likely, pass out drunk. The minute Cleon get a one-man show and start gettin' reviewed by the *Times-Picayune*, he decide he a celebrity and he like that fine. He go out every night with his no account friends and he argue about art and politics—and he get interviewed by magazines, and all of a sudden he look around and notice he got so many women after him, ain' no way he can get aroun' to 'em all.

Tha's Cleon. Me, I stay home and paint. Now, seems like he got the better part of the bargain, but mostly I like my life and Cleon don't like his. Because he know he livin' a lie. So the more I work and enjoy my work, the more he got to put me down.

Meanwhile, he gettin' so famous, all kind of celebrities start wantin' him to paint they portraits. He make the appointments, go out to lunch and dinner with 'em, take me along "to take notes" while he do his "preliminary sketches," while, really, I be the one makin' the sketches.

You'd think that'd be humiliatin' enough, but he got to bring women around. He start doin' that and I get mad just like I'm s'posed to and finally he start havin' a thing with Sondra Bartell. Yes ma'am, that Sondra Bartell. Maybe the best vocalist this country has ever produced since Billie Holiday herself. I'll tell you, I was mighty thrilled to do that job. Then, Cleon break my heart. Tha's right—he had women before, and lots of 'em. But he didn't have no hot love affair right in front of my eyes with maybe the number one person I admire in this world.

He really want to make me feel bad about it, so he tell her he gon' need several sketchin' sessions and he make me go with him, watch her come love on him just like I wasn't there. Come put her arms aroun' his neck and look at his little first grade drawings, pretend like she think they good; then he kiss her, nuzzle her neck, and me just sittin' there.

Did she know I was his wife? Why, yes, Officer, she did, and she just didn't care. Well, you right, Officer. I shouldn'ta put up with it. I shoulda just walk on out of there.

And the first time it happen we had a big old scene afterward, end with Cleon sayin' how much he love me, I'm the only woman he really want, and then gettin' all romantic— tryin' to, anyway. But he get too drunk and fall asleep before he get around to anything. Ha! Jus' like always.

Second time it happen, I do walk out. Walk right over to my lawyer's office and say I want to file for divorce. I don't need this shit—we got community property laws in this state; with only half what I made paintin' pictures over the years I figure I can be a wealthy woman. Don't need no Cleon Banks, right, Officer? Wrong.

What I didn't know is Cleon went and "invested" the money. Invested in what, I don't know. Wine, women and song, maybe.

No, I oughta be fair. Gave some to his brother for his plumbin' business—brother's doin' fine now, thank you. Then some other friend start up a restaurant—you know how many restaurants succeed and how many fail? Tha's right— and this one in the "fail" category. Anyway, buncha things like that. So we got no bank account.

Well, still no problem. What we do have is a whole basement full o' pictures ain't been sold yet—probably half a million dollars down there; maybe more. But meanwhile, I moved out to this little place, and Cleon got control of the basement.

Tha's right, Officer. Put your head on the table and cover your ears. 'Cause you know what's comin' next. Suddenly, those pictures can't be found.

What's that? Well, 'course I testify that I'm the one paint the pictures. And Cleon, he testify that I already lie about the pictures in the basement, I'm crazy and always have been, I'm the one who drink, and I'm the one havin' affairs. You name it, he say it.

So my lawyer say he gon' prove I'm the real artist; we gon' have a paintin' contest right there in court. I'm gon' paint a Dancin' Man picture and Cleon gon' paint one and then we gon' get a art critic to express his opinion right in front of the judge.

Well, the judge won't go for it. Cleon lawyer call it a frivolous claim and the judge go for that instead. No, the judge wasn't white. Funny question for you to ask—you white as rice yourself. I b'lieve if the judge had been white, I'd'a had a better chance. This man like Cleon. They two of a kind; got the two biggest dicks in town. That judge didn't have no use for me; none atall. Cleon his main man.

So we divide up all the property in sight which, at this point, consists of nothin' but the house. And the house, because of certain business deals Cleon didn't bother to tell me about, turns out to have a third mortgage on it.

That leave me with about enough money to pay my lawyer, and Cleon with half a million dollars in paintings which he can now claim he producin' right along. Maybe he's even gon' say he cuttin' down his production so they go up in value. But then he's s'posed to give me spousal support, so maybe he's gon' sell 'em privately—not even go through Dahveed. That probably double the value of 'em, and there wouldn't be no record of the sales. So he wouldn't owe me anything. Oh, yeah, I wouldn't put nothin' past Cleon.

Meanwhile, I got no income.

So, here's what I do. I say to Cleon, look, you need me for one last thing and I need money real bad, so you come on over and let's talk about it. I tell him I might do that portrait of Sondra Bartell if he'll let me have the money for it.

Well, I know I got him—'cause he need the portrait to keep her interested. But of course he gon' try to argue down the price, say he should get half. So he pass by, and he standin' on the porch, lookin' real scared. And I say, oh, come on in and have a drink. Well, that's a invitation Cleon never could resist.

So I give him a drink and Cleon say, "Baby, we sho' did have some good times, didn't we?"

Officer? Officer, you okay? You need a damp cloth or anything? I'm used to it, see—I live with the man twenty-five years. I know what he's like.

So I say, "Yes, Lord, we sure did." And I start to reminisce with him. Meanwhile, he have another drink, then another. Pretty soon he start gettin' flirtatious.

You say somethin', Officer? Well, yeah, he got a lot of nerve. But I jus' told you—he think his dick so big you can't hardly get in the room with him. So I flirt back and pretty soon he start kissin' on me. I say, "Cleon, honey, I ain't had none of that in a long time. How 'bout we get in bed and talk some more?" So we do, and he say, "This is a mighty fine new brass bed you got." And sure enough it is—the kind with brass bars at the top and more at the bottom.

And I say, "I was thinkin' of you when I bought it."

And then I say, "Why don' you let me rub ya back, baby?" So he turn over and I get started and pretty soon, I hear snorin'.

Yeah, you right, Officer: Just like I knew I was goin' to.

Well, you figured out the rest already, ain't you? I already got just the right bed so I could handcuff his hands to the headboard and his feet to the footboard. So I go ahead and do it.

And then I paint Sondra Bartell right on his butt. I put her face right in the one place he couldn't put it himself. Uh-uh, I think I'm gon' have another laughin' fit.

Woo. 'Scuse me, Officer. Sure did feel good. Didn't it? I notice you crackin' a smile your own self.

Well, anyway, once I get my paintin' done, I call up a few friends in the press I happen to know from my divorce trial and they record that picture once for all for God and everybody.

I bet now I'm back in the paintin' business, what do you think? Oh, yeah, sure—I am if I manage to beat the rap on this.

Why, no, he didn't wake up all the time I was paintin'. Not even while the reporters was here.

Yeah, he sleep pretty sound most of the time. What's that?

'Course I didn't put nothin' in his drink.

Oh, wait a minute—wait a minute, now. I jus' remember somethin'. Come to think of it, he say he got a little cold, and I did see him take a couple of pills. Not sure what they was, Officer; but I know gon' find the rest of 'em in his pants pocket.

You smilin' again, Officer? I didn't know you had it in ya.

Yeah, I did wash those glasses. I'm a pretty tidy person— tha's one reason I was such a good wife.

Unfortunate thing, though—one of 'em broke on me. Had to throw away the pieces.

Well, looka there—here come the medics. I guess they'll prob'ly want to pump his stomach. He be all right, though. Like I say—I'm a pretty tidy person.

Well, now, thanks, Officer. Good luck with your career, too. Why, sure. I'd be glad to paint you sometime. You can be my second client.

Blood Types

"Refresh my recollection, counsellor. Are holographic wills legal in California?"

Though we'd hardly spoken in seven years or more, I recognized the voice on the phone as easily if I'd heard it yesterday. I'd lived with its owner once. "Gary Wilder. Aren't you feeling well?"

"I feel fine. Settle a bet, okay?"

"Unless you slept through more classes than I thought, you know perfectly well they're legal."

"They used to be. It's been a long time, you know? How are you, Rebecca?"

"Great. And you're a daddy, I hear. How's Stephanie?"

"Fine."

"And the wee one?"

"Little Laurie-bear. The best thing that ever happened to me."

"You sound happy."

"Laurie's my life."

I was sorry to hear it. That was a lot of responsibility for a ten-month-old.

"So about the will," Gary continued. "Have the rules changed since we were at Boalt?"

"A bit. Remember how it could be invalidated by anything pre-printed on it? Like in that case where there was a date stamped on the paper the woman used, and the whole thing was thrown out?"

"Yeah. I remember someone asked whether you could use your own letterhead."

"That was you, Gary."

"Probably. And you couldn't, it seems to me."

"But you probably could now. Now only the 'materially relevant' part has to be handwritten. And you don't have to date it."

"No? That seems odd."

"Well, you would if there were a previous dated will. Otherwise just write it out, sign it, and it's legal."

Something about the call, maybe just the melancholy of hearing a voice from the past, put me in a gray and restless mood. It was mid-December and pouring outside—perfect weather for doleful ruminations on a man I hardly knew any more. I couldn't help worrying that if Laurie was Gary's whole life, that didn't speak well for his marriage. Shouldn't Stephanie at least have gotten a small mention? But she hadn't and the Gary I knew could easily have fallen out of love with her. He was one of life's stationary drifters—staying in the same place, but drifting from one mild interest to another, none of them very consuming and none very durable. I hoped it would be different with Laurie; it wouldn't be easy to watch your dad wimp out on you.

But I sensed it was already happening. I suspected that phone call meant little Laurie, who was his life, was making him feel tied down and he was sending out feelers to former and future lady friends.

The weather made me think of a line from a poem Gary used to quote:

> "Il pleure dans mon coeur
> Comme il pleut sur la ville."

He was the sort to quote Paul Verlaine. He read everything, retained everything, and didn't do much. He had never
finished law school, had sold insurance for awhile and was
now dabbling in real estate, I'd heard, though I didn't know
what that meant, exactly. Probably trying to figure out a way
to speculate with Stephanie's money, which, out of affection
for Gary, I thanked heaven she had. If you can't make up your
mind what to do with your life, you should at least marry well
and waffle in comfort.

Gary died that night. Reading about it in the morning
Chronicle, I shivered, thinking the phone call was one of those
grisly coincidences. But the will came the next day.

The *Chronicle* story said Gary and Stephanie were both
killed instantly when their car went over a cliff on a twisty
road in a blinding rainstorm. The rains were hellish that year.
It was the third day of a five-day flood.

Madeline Bell, a witness to the accident, said Gary had
swerved to avoid hitting her Mercedes as she came round a
curve. The car had exploded and burned as Bell watched it
roll off a hill near San Anselmo, where Stephanie and Gary
lived.

Even in that moment of shock I think I felt more grief for
Laurie than I did for Gary, who had half-lived his life at best.
Only a day before, when I'd talked to Gary, Laurie had had it
made—her mama was rich and her daddy good-looking. Now
she was an orphan.

I wondered where Gary and Stephanie were going in such
an awful storm. To a party, probably, or home from one. It
was the height of the holiday season.

I knew Gary's mother, of course. Would she already be at
the Wilder house, for Hanukkah, perhaps? If not, she'd be
coming soon; I'd call in a day or two.

In the meantime, I called Rob Burns, who had long since replaced Gary in my affections, and asked to see him that night. I hadn't thought twice of Gary in the past five years, but something was gone from my life and I needed comfort. It would be good to sleep with Rob by my side and the sound of rain on the roof—life-affirming, as we say in California. I'd read somewhere that Mark Twain, when he built his mansion in Hartford, installed a section of tin roof so as to get the best rain sounds. I could understand the impulse.

It was still pouring by mid-morning the next day, and my throat was feeling slightly scratchy, the way it does when a cold's coming on. I was rummaging for Vitamin C when Kruzick brought the mail in—Alan Kruzick, incredibly inept but inextricably installed secretary for the law firm of Nicholson and Schwartz, of which I was a protesting partner. The other partner, Chris Nicholson, liked his smart-ass style, my sister Mickey was his girl friend, and my mother had simply laid down the law—hire him and keep him.

"Any checks?" I asked.

"Nope. Nothing interesting but a letter from a dead man."

"What?"

He held up an envelope with Gary Wilder's name and address in the upper left corner. "Maybe he wants you to channel him."

The tears that popped into my eyes quelled even Kruzick.

The will was in Gary's own handwriting, signed, written on plain paper, and dated December 17, the day of Gary's death. It said:

"This is my last will and testament, superseding all others. I leave everything I own to my daughter, Laurie Wilder. If my wife and I die before her 21st birthday, I appoint my brother, Michael Wilder, as her legal guardian. I also appoint my brother as executor of this will."

My stomach clutched as I realized that Gary had known when we talked that he and Stephanie were in danger. He'd managed to seem his usual happy-go-lucky self, using the trick he had of hiding his feelings that had made him hard to live with.

But if he knew he was going to be killed, why hadn't he given the murderer's identity? Perhaps he had, I realized. I was a lawyer, so I'd gotten the will. Someone else might have gotten a letter about what was happening. I wondered if my old boy friend had gotten involved with the dope trade. After all, he lived in Marin County, which had the highest population of coke dealers outside the greater Miami area.

I phoned Gary's brother at his home in Seattle, but was told he'd gone to San Anselmo. I had a client coming in five minutes, but after that, nothing pressing. And so, by two o'clock I was on the Golden Gate Bridge, enjoying a rare moment of foggy overcast, the rain having relented for awhile.

It was odd about Gary's choosing Michael for Laurie's guardian. When I'd known him well he'd had nothing but contempt for his brother. Michael was a stockbroker and a go-getter; Gary was a mooner-about, a romantic, and a rebel. He considered his brother boring, stuffy, a bit crass and utterly worthless. On the other hand, he adored his sister, Jeri, a free-spirited dental hygienist married to a good-natured sometime carpenter.

Was Michael married? Yes, I thought. At least he had been. Maybe fatherhood had changed Gary's opinions on what was important—Michael's money and stability might have looked good to him when he thought of sending Laurie to college.

I pulled up in front of the Wilder-Cooper house, a modest redwood one that had probably cost nearly half a million. Such were real estate values in Marin County—and such was Stephanie's bank account.

At home were Michael Wilder—wearing a suit—and Stephanie's parents, Mary and Jack Cooper. Mary was a big woman, comfortable and talkative; Jack was skinny and withdrawn. He stared into space, almost sad, but mostly just faraway, and I got the feeling watching TV was his great passion in life, though perhaps he drank as well. The idea, it appeared, was simply to leave the room without anyone noticing, the means of transportation being entirely insignificant.

It was a bit awkward, my being the ex-girl friend and showing up unexpectedly. Michael didn't seem to know how to introduce me, and I could take a hint. It was no time to ask to see him privately.

"I'd hoped to see your mother," I said.

"She's at the hospital," said Mary. "We're taking turns now that—" she started to cry.

"The hospital!"

"You don't know about Laurie?"

"She was in the accident?"

"No. She's been very ill for the last two months."

"Near death," said Mary. "What that child has been through shouldn't happen to an animal. Tiny little face just contorts itself like a poor little monkey's. Screams and screams and screams; and rivers flow out of her little bottom. Rivers, Miss Schwartz!"

Her shoulders hunched and began to shake. Michael looked helpless. Mechanically, Jack put an arm around her.

"What's wrong?" I asked Michael.

He shrugged. "They don't know. Can't diagnose it."

"Now, Mary," said Jack. "She's better. The doctor said so last night."

"What hospital is she in?"

"Marin General."

I said to Michael: "I think I'll pop by and see your mother—would you mind pointing me in the right direction? I've got a map in the car."

When we arrived at the curb, I said, "I can find the hospital. I wanted to give you something."

I handed him the will. "This came in today's mail. It'll be up to you as executor to petition the court for probate." As he read, a look of utter incredulity came over his face. "But—I'm divorced. I can't take care of a baby."

"Gary didn't ask in advance if you'd be willing?"

"Yes, but—I didn't think he was going to die!" His voice got higher as reality caught up with him. "He called the day of the accident. But I thought he was just depressed. You know how people get around the holidays."

"What did he say exactly?"

"He said he had this weird feeling, that's all—like something bad might happen to him. And would I take care of Laurie if anything did."

"He didn't say he was scared? In any kind of trouble?"

"No—just feeling weird."

"Michael, he wasn't dealing, was he?"

"Are you kidding? I'd be the last to know." He looked at the ground a minute. "I guess he could have been."

Ellen Wilder was cooing to Laurie when I got to the hospital. "Ohhhh, she's much better now. She just needed her Grandma's touch, that's all it was."

She spoke to the baby in the third person, unaware I was there until I announced myself, whereupon she almost dropped the precious angel-wangel. We had a tearful reunion, Gary's mother and I. We both missed Gary and we both felt for poor Laurie.

Ellen adored the baby more than breath, to listen to her,

and not only that, she possessed the healing power of a witch. She had spent the night Gary and Stephanie were killed with Laurie, and all day the next day, never even going home for a shower. And gradually, the fever had broken, metaphorically speaking. With Grandma's loving attention, the baby's debilitating diarrhea had begun to ease off and little Laurie had seemed to come back to life.

"Look, Rebecca." She tiptoed to the sleeping baby. "See those cheeks? Roses in them. She's getting her pretty color back, widdle Waurie is, yes, her is." She seemed not to realize she'd lapsed into babytalk.

She came back and sat down beside me. "Stephanie stayed with her nearly round the clock, you know. She was the best mother anyone ever—" Ellen teared up for a second and glanced round the room, embarrassed.

"Look. She left her clothes here. I'll have to remember to take them home. The best mother . . . she and Gary were invited to a party that night. It was a horrible rainy, rainy night, but poor Stephanie hadn't been anywhere but the hospital in weeks—"

"How long had you been here?"

"Oh, just a few days. I came for Hanukkah—and to help out if I could. I knew Stephanie had to get out, so I offered to stay with Laurie. I was just dying to have some time with the widdle fweet fing anyhow—" This last was spoken more or less in Laurie's direction. Ellen seemed to have developed a habit of talking to the child while carrying on other conversations.

"What happened was Gary had quite a few drinks before he brought me over. Oh, God, I never should have let him drive! We nearly had a wreck on the way over—you know how stormy it was. I kept telling him he was too drunk to drive, and he said I wanted it that way, just like I always wanted him to have strep throat when he was a kid. He said he felt fine then and he felt fine now."

I was getting lost. "You wanted him to have strep throat?"

She shrugged. "I don't know what he meant. He was just drunk, that's all. Oh, God, my poor baby!" She sniffed, fumbled in her purse, and blew her nose into a tissue.

"Did he seem okay that day—except for being drunk?"

"Fine. Why?"

"He called me that afternoon—about his will. And he called Michael to say he—well, I guess to say he had a premonition about his death."

"His will? He called you about a will?"

"Yes."

"But he and Stephanie had already made their wills. Danny Goldstein drew them up." That made sense, as Gary had dated his holograph. Danny had been at Boalt with Gary and me. I wondered briefly if it hurt Ellen to be reminded that all Gary's classmates had gone on to become lawyers just like their parents would have wanted.

A fresh-faced nurse popped in and took a look at Laurie. "How's our girl?"

"Like a different baby."

The nurse smiled. "She sure is. We were really worried for awhile there." But the smile faded almost instantly. "It's so sad. I never saw a more devoted mother. Laurie never needed us at all—Stephanie was her nurse. One of the best I ever saw."

"I didn't know Stephanie was a nurse." The last I'd heard she was working part-time for a caterer, trying to make up her mind whether to go to chef's school. Stephanie had a strong personality, but she wasn't much more career-minded than Gary was. Motherhood, everyone seemed to think, had been her true calling.

"She didn't have any training—she was just good with infants. You should have seen the way she'd sit and rock that child for hours, Laurie having diarrhea so bad she hardly had any skin on her little butt, crying her little heart out. She must have been in agony like you and I couldn't imagine. But finally Stephanie would get her to sleep. Nobody else could."

"Nobody else could breast-feed her," I said, thinking surely I'd hit on the source of Stephanie's amazing talent.

"Stephanie couldn't either. Didn't have enough milk." The nurse shrugged. "Anyone can give a bottle. It wasn't that."

When she left, I said, "I'd better go. Can I do anything for you?"

Ellen thought a minute. "You know what you could do? Will you be going by Gary's again?"

"I'd be glad to."

"You could take some of Stephanie's clothes and things. They're going to let Laurie out in a day or two and there's so much stuff here." She looked exasperated.

Glad to help, I gathered up clothes and began to fold them. Ellen found a canvas carry-all of Stephanie's to pack them in. Zipping it open, I saw a bit of white powder in the bottom, and my stomach flopped over. I couldn't get the notion of drugs out of my mind. Gary had had a "premonition—" of death, the kind you might get if you burned someone and they threatened you—and now I was looking at white powder.

I found some plastic bags in a drawer that had probably once been used to transport diapers or formula and lined the bottom of the carryall with them, to keep the powder from sticking to Stephanie's clothes.

But instead of going to Gary's, I dropped in at my parents' house in San Rafael. It was about four o'clock and I had some phoning to do before five.

"Darling!" said Mom. "Isn't it awful about poor Gary Wilder?"

Mom had always liked Gary. She had a soft spot for ne'er-do-wells, as I knew only too well. She was the main reason Kruzick was currently ruining my life. The person for whom she hadn't a minute was the one I preferred most—the blue-eyed and dashing Mr. Rob Burns, star reporter for the San Francisco Chronicle.

Using the phone in my dad's study, Rob was the very person I rang up. His business was asking questions that were none of his business, and I had a few for him to ask.

Quickly explaining the will, the odd phone call to Michael, and the white powder, I had him hooked. He smelled the same rat I smelled and, more important, he smelled a story.

While he made his calls, I phoned Danny Goldstein. "Becky baby!"

"Don't call me that."

"Terrible about Gary, isn't it? Makes you think, man."

"Terrible about Stephanie too."

"I don't know. She pussy-whipped him."

"She was better than Melissa."

Danny laughed unkindly, brayed you could even say. Everyone knew Gary had left me for Melissa, who was twenty-two and a cutesy-wootsy dollbaby who couldn't be trusted to go to the store for a six-pack. Naturally, everyone thought I had Gary pussy-whipped when the truth was, he wouldn't brush his teeth without asking my advice about it. He was a man desperate for a woman to run his life and I was relieved to be rid of the job.

But still, Melissa had hurt my pride. I thought Gary's choosing her meant he'd grown up and no longer needed me. It was a short-lived maturity, however—within two years

Stephanie had appeared on the scene. I might not see it exactly the way Danny did, but I had to admit if he'd had any balls, she was the one to bust them.

"I hear motherhood mellowed her," I said.

"Yeah, she was born for it. Always worrying was the kid too hot, too cold, too hungry—one of those poo-poo moms."

"Huh?"

"You know. Does the kid want to go poo-poo? Did the kid already go poo-poo? Does it go poo-poo enough? Does it go poo-poo too much? Is it going poo-poo right now? She could discuss color and consistency through a whole dinner party, salmon mousse to kiwi tart."

I laughed. Who didn't know the type? "Say listen, Danny," I said. "Did you know Laurie's been in the hospital?"

"Yeah. Marina, my wife, went to see Stephanie—tried to get her to go out and get some air while she took care of the baby, but Stephanie wouldn't budge."

"I hear you drew up Gary and Stephanie's wills."

"Yeah. God, I never thought—poor little Laurie. They asked Gary's sister to be her guardian—he hated his brother and Stephanie was an only child."

"Guess what? Gary made another will just before he died, naming the brother as Laurie's guardian."

"I don't believe it."

"Believe it. I'll send you a copy."

"There's going to be a hell of a court fight."

I wasn't so sure about that. The court, of course, wouldn't be bound by either parent's nomination. Since Gary's will nominated Jeri as guardian, she and Michael might choose to fight it out, but given Michael's apparent hesitation to take Laurie, I wasn't sure there'd be any argument at all.

"Danny," I said, "you were seeing a lot of him, right?"

"Yeah. We played racquetball."

"Was he dealing coke? Or something else?"

"Gary? No way. You can't be a dealer and be as broke as he was."

The phone rang almost the minute I hung up. Rob had finished a round of calls to what he called "his law enforcement sources." He'd learned that Gary's brakes hadn't been tampered with, handily blowing my murder theory.

Or seemingly blowing it. Something was still very wrong, and I wasn't giving up till I knew what the powder was. Mom asked me to dinner, but I headed back to the city—Rob had said he could get someone to run an analysis that night.

It was raining again by the time I'd dropped the stuff off, refused Rob's dinner invitation (that was two) and gone home to solitude and split pea soup that I make up in advance and keep in the freezer for nights like this. It was the second night after Gary's death. The first night I'd needed to reassure myself I was still alive; now I needed to mourn. I didn't plan anything fancy like sackcloth and ashes, just a quiet night home with a book, free to let my mind wander and my eyes fill up from time to time.

But first I had a message from Michael Wilder. He wanted to talk. He felt awful, calling me like this, but there was no one in his family he felt he could talk to. Couldn't we meet for coffee or something?

Sure we could—at my house. Not even for Gary's brother was I going out in the rain again.

After the soup, I showered and changed into jeans. Michael arrived in wool slacks and a sportcoat—not even in repose, apparently, did he drop the stuffy act. Maybe life with Laurie would loosen him up. I asked if he'd thought any more about being her guardian.

It flustered him. "Not really," he said, and didn't meet my eyes.

"I found out the original wills named Jeri as guardian. If Stephanie didn't make a last-minute one too, hers will still be in effect. Meaning Jeri could fight you if you decide you want Laurie."

"I can't even imagine being a father," he said. "But Gary must have had a good reason . . ." he broke off. "Poor little kid. A week ago everyone thought she was the one who was going to die."

"What's wrong with her—besides diarrhea?" I realized I hadn't had the nerve to ask either of the grandmothers because I knew exactly what would happen—I'd get details that would give me symptoms and two hours later, maybe three or four, I'd be backing towards the door, nodding, with a glazed look on my face, watching matriarchal jaws continue to work.

But Michael only grimaced. "That's all I know about—just life-threatening diarrhea."

"Life-threatening?"

"Without an IV, a dehydrated baby can die in fifteen minutes. Just ask my mother." He shrugged. "Anyway, the doctors talked about electrolyte abnormalities, whatever they may be, and did every test in the book. But the only thing they found was what they called 'high serum sodium levels'." He shrugged again, as if to shake something off. "Don't ask—especially don't ask my mom or Stephanie's."

We both laughed. I realized Michael had good reasons for finding sudden parenthood a bit on the daunting side.

I got us some wine and when I came back, he'd turned deadly serious. "Rebecca, something weird happened today. Look what I found." He held out a paper signed by Gary and headed "Beneficiary Designation." "Know what that is?"

I shook my head.

"I used to be in insurance—as did my little brother. It's the form you use to change your life insurance beneficiary."

The form was dated December 16, the day before Gary's death. Michael had been named beneficiary and Laurie contingent beneficiary. Michael said, "Pretty weird, huh?"

I nodded.

"I also found both Gary's and Stephanie's policies—each for half a million dollars and each naming the other as beneficiary, with Laurie as contingent. For some reason, Gary went to see his insurance agent the day before he died and changed his. What do you make of it?"

I didn't at all like what I made of it. "It goes with the will," I said. "He named you as Laurie's guardian, so he must have wanted to make sure you could afford to take care of her."

"I could afford it. For Christ's sake!"

"He must have wanted to compensate you." I stopped for a minute. "It might be his way of saying thanks."

"You're avoiding the subject, aren't you?"

I was. "You mean it would have made more sense to leave the money to Laurie directly."

"Yes. Unless he'd provided for her some other way."

"Stephanie had money."

"I don't think Gary knew how much, though."

I took a sip of wine and thought about it, or rather thought about ways to talk about it, because it was beginning to look very ugly. "You're saying you think," I said carefully, "that he knew she was going to inherit the half million from Stephanie's policy. Because she was going to die and he was the beneficiary and he was going to die and his new will left his own property to Laurie."

Michael was blunt: "It looks like murder-suicide, doesn't it?"

I said, "Yeah," unable to say any more.

Michael took me over ground I'd already mentally covered: "He decided to do it in a hurry, probably because it was raining so hard—an accident in the rain would be much more plausible. He made the arrangements. Then he called me and muttered about a premonition, to give himself some sort of feeble motive for suddenly getting his affairs in order; he may have said the same thing to other people as well. Finally, he pretended to be drunk, made a big show of almost having an accident on the way to the hospital, picked up Stephanie and drove her over a cliff."

Still putting things together, I mumbled, "You couldn't really be sure you'd die going over just any cliff. You'd have to pick the right cliff, wouldn't you?" And then I said, "I wonder if the insurance company will figure it out."

"Oh, who cares! He probably expected they would but wanted to make the gesture. And he knew I didn't need the money. That's not the point. The point is why?" He stood up and ran his fingers through his hair, working off excess energy. "Why kill himself, Rebecca? And why take Stephanie with him?"

"I don't know," I said. But I hadn't a doubt that that was what he'd done. There was another why—why make Michael Laurie's guardian? Why not his sister as originally planned?

The next day was Saturday and I would have dozed happily into mid-morning if Rob hadn't phoned at eight. "You know the sinister white powder?"

"Uh-huh."

"Baking soda."

"That's all?"

"That's it. No heroin, no cocaine, not even any baby talc. Baking soda. Period."

I thanked him and turned over, but the next couple of

hours were full of vaguely disquieting dreams. I woke upset, feeling oddly tainted, as if I'd collaborated in Gary's crimes. It wasn't till I was in the shower—performing my purification ritual if you believe in such things—that things came together in my conscious mind. The part of me that dreamed had probably known all along.

I called a doctor friend to find out if what I suspected made medical sense. It did: to a baby Laurie's age, baking soda would be a deadly poison. Simply add it to the formula, and the excess sodium would cause her to develop severe dehydrating diarrhea; it might ultimately lead to death. But she would be sick only as long as someone continued to doctor her formula. The poisoning was not cumulative; as soon as it stopped, she would begin to recover and in only a few days she would be dramatically better.

In other words, he described Laurie's illness to a T. And Stephanie, the world's greatest mother, who was there round the clock, must have fed her—at any rate would have had all the opportunity in the world to doctor her formula.

It didn't make sense. Well, part of it did. The part I could figure out was this: Gary saw Stephanie put baking soda in the formula, already knew about the high sodium reports, put two and two together, may or not have confronted her . . . no, definitely didn't confront her. Gary never confronted anyone.

He simply came to the conclusion that his wife was poisoning their child and decided to kill her, taking his own aimless life as well. That would account for the hurry—to stop the poisoning without having to confront Stephanie. If he accused her, he might be able to stop her, but things would instantly get far too messy for Gary-the-conflict-avoider. Worse, the thing could easily become a criminal case and if Stephanie were convicted, Laurie would have to grow up knowing her mother had deliberately poisoned her. If she were acquitted, Laurie might always be in danger. I could follow his benighted reasoning perfectly.

But I couldn't, for all the garlic in Gilroy, imagine why Stephanie would want to kill Laurie. By all accounts, she was the most of loving of mothers, would probably even have laid down her own life for her child's. I called a shrink friend, Elaine Alvarez.

"Of course she loved the child," Elaine explained. "Why shouldn't she? Laurie perfectly answered her needs." And then she told me some things that made me forget I'd been planning to consume a large breakfast in a few minutes. On the excuse of finally remembering to take Stephanie's clothes, I drove to Gary's house.

The family was planning a memorial service in a day or two for the dead couple; Jeri had just arrived at her dead brother's house; friends had dropped by to comfort the bereaved; yet there was almost a festive atmosphere in the house. Laurie had come home that morning.

Michael and I took a walk. "Bullshit!" he said. "Dogcrap! No one could have taken better care of that baby than Stephanie. Christ, she martyred herself. She stayed up night after night . . ."

"Listen to yourself. Everything you're saying confirms what Elaine told me. The thing even has a name. It's called Munchausen Syndrome by Proxy. The original syndrome, plain old Munchausen, is when you hurt or mutilate yourself to get attention.

" 'By proxy' means you do it to your nearest and dearest. People say, 'Oh, that poor woman. God, what she's been through. Look how brave she is! Why, no one in the world could be a better mother.' And Mom gets off on it. There are recorded cases of it, Michael, at least one involving a mother and baby."

He was pale. "I think I'm going to throw up."

"Let's sit down a minute."

In fact, stuffy, uptight Michael ended up lying down in the dirt on the side of the road, nice flannel slacks and all, taking breaths till his color returned. And then, slowly, we walked back to the house.

Jeri was holding Laurie, her mother standing over her, Mary Cooper sitting close on the couch. "Oh, look what a baby-waby. What a darling girly-wirl. Do you feel the least bit hot? Laurie-baurie, you're not running a fever, are you?"

The kid had just gotten the thumbs-up from a hospital and she was wrapped in half a dozen blankets. I doubted she was running a fever.

Ellen leaned over to feel the baby's face. "Ohhh, I think she might be. Give her to Grandma. Grandma knows how to fix babies, doesn't she, Laurie girl? Come to Grandma and Grandma will sponge you with alcohol, Grandma will."

She looked like a hawk coming in for a landing, ready to snare its prey and fly up again, but Mary was quicker still. Almost before you saw it happening, she had the baby away from Ellen and in her own lap. "What you need is some nice juice, don't you Laurie-bear? And then Meemaw's going to rock you and rock you . . . oh, my goodness, you're burning up." Her voice was on the edge of panic. "Listen, Jeri, this baby's wheezing! We're got to get her breathing damp air . . ."

She wasn't wheezing, she was gulping, probably in amazement. I felt my own jaw drop and, looking away, unwittingly caught the eye of Mary's husband, who hadn't wanted me to see the anguish there. Quickly, he dropped a curtain of blandness. Beside me, I heard Michael whisper, "My God!"

I knew we were seeing something extreme. They were all excited to have Laurie home and they were competing with each other, letting out what looked like their scariest sides if you knew what we did. But a Stephanie didn't come along every day. Laurie was in no further danger, I was sure of it. Still, I understood why Gary had had the sudden change of heart about her guardianship.

I turned to Michael. "Are you going to try to get her?"

He plucked at his sweater sleeve, staring at his wrist as if it had a treasure map on it. "I haven't decided."

An image from my fitful morning dreams came back to me: a giant in a forest, taller than all the trees and built like a mountain; a female giant with belly and breasts like boulders, dressed in white robes and carrying, draped across her out-stretched arms, a dead man, head dangling on its flaccid neck.

In a few days Michael called. When he got home to Seattle, a letter had been waiting for him—a note, rather, from Gary, postmarked the day of his death. It didn't apologize, it didn't explain—it didn't even say, "Dear Michael." It was simply a quote from Hamlet typed on a piece of paper, not handwritten, Michael thought, because it could be construed as a confession and there was the insur-ance to think about.

This was the quote:

> Diseases desperate grown
> By desperate appliance are relieved,
> Or not at all.

I didn't ask Michael again whether he intended to take Laurie. I was too furious, at the moment, with one passive male, to trust myself to speak civilly with another. Instead, I simmered inwardly, thinking how like Gary it was to confess to murder with a quote from Shakespeare. Thinking that, as he typed it, he probably imagined grandly that nothing in his life would become him like the leaving of it. The schmuck.

Always Othello

Detective Skip Langdon, New Orleans P. D., lived in the thick of the French Quarter, and figured she was probably the only cop in the parish who did. Cops, she'd observed, were suburbanites at heart, like most of the folks in the Third District, to which she'd been recently assigned.

After working Homicide, it sometimes seemed to Skip the Third was only technically in the city. There was a housing project, but a smallish one. Most folks lived in nice subdivisions by the lake, and on the manicured streets of Gentilly (which also has a tough side, but everything is relative).

When "decentralization" came, homicide detectives became "gen dicks", or general detectives, and in the Third, there weren't that many homicides, anyway.

Yet Skip was staring down at a corpse in a living room in a part of Gentilly that has streets so nasty-neat you want to call a graffiti artist just to get comfortable. The living room was in a Spanish style house that looked like it had run saway from Florida. The corpse had a hole in its chest.

Ironic, she thought. This is one of those neighborhoods where it just doesn't happen—according to the residents.

The body on the floor was that of a woman, a young woman, somewhere in the neighborhood of thirty, tall and thin, with long, elegant legs poking out of a pair of plaid cotton shorts, which she had paired with a white T-shirt. She wore no shoes. She had golden blonde shoulder length hair, and Skip's first thought was that she was a beautiful young woman. Yet she hadn't really looked at the face, had merely taken in the facts of death, and woman, and young.

Neither Skip nor her sergeant, Adam Abasolo, was in a hurry to call an ambulance, as the massive quantity of blood on the beige wall-to-wall was congealed and nearly brown. The woman's body was dead white, showing that what blood she still had in her had had time to pool on the other side of her body. Officially, neither Skip nor Abasolo could pronounce her, but they knew dead when they saw it. Skip took time to look at the woman closely. "Omigod—I know her. She's my neighbor."

"Since when did you move to Gentilly?" Abasolo sounded genuinely puzzled.

Wildly, Skip glanced around. "Well, I guess she does live here. I always assumed . . . I mean, she's such a French Quarter type."

"Who is she, Skip?"

"She goes by Franny Futura. Damn! I'm going to miss her."

She knew she would feel Franny's death nearly as intently as if she'd been a friend. Franny was a French Quarter character, as much a fixture in Skip's life, and the lives of her neighbors, as Jackson Square itself, where Franny read the Tarot.

The Tarot readers had recently become at least as prominent as the artists and musicians who hung at the square—indeed had taken to feuding with the latter, on grounds they couldn't communicate with their customers while "The Saints" wailed two feet away.

There must have been twenty of them, at least, and they all knew they had only a minute to catch the eye of the strolling tourist. Thus the man with the purple hair had a sign proclaiming him a member of Mensa; Hubba-Bubba wore a red cloak and sequined gold headdress (and weighed close to a quarter of a ton); The Mystic Begeleh was a dachshund who spoke through his human companion; and Starlady's tulle-trimmed hat probably measured more than two feet across.

You had to be colorful to get noticed in that crowd.

And Franny was. She'd somehow hit on a mix of the retro, the futuristic, and the outrageous that made you giggle whether you wanted to or not. Her garments, clearly meant to simulate some imagined spacesuit fabric, were silver. But instead of being fashioned into a little mini number suitable for Princess Leia, they were eminently ladylike (if you didn't count the plunging neckline). The top was a simple sleeveless blouse, plunging as mentioned, and tucked into a tight calf-length skirt, to form an outfit that would have been smart with hat and gloves.

Franny didn't disappoint. The gloves, also silver, were shirred and pearl-buttoned. They had cut-out fingers that allowed her to lay out the cards.

But the hat was what made the outfit. About half the diameter of Starlady's, it was a flat silver disk with a hut-shaped knob on top. Can you picture it? A perfect stylized '50s flying saucer perched atop her perfect golden pageboy. She was so tall and thin and elegant some said she was a drag queen.

Now she was queen of nothing.

Abasolo called the crime lab and the coroner while Skip surveyed the house. She couldn't touch anything yet, but she could look.

And the house will speak to me, she thought. It will give up Franny's secrets. Houses had a way of doing that. A full liquor cabinet, for instance, spoke volumes next to a shelf of Twelve-Step books.

The first thing she noticed was that Franny had spent bucks here—or someone had. Except for the body on the floor and a water stain where the roof had leaked, the living room looked pretty good. Over the carpet, there was a small, Belgian-made oriental rug, and there was new, decent furniture, the kind that comes in a "set"—ordinary but presentable. The other rooms were furnished more or less with odds and ends. A bit haphazard, Skip thought, but it wasn't shabby for someone who made a living in flying saucer drag.

Skip wondered if Franny lived here alone, or if she were married; or if she really was a drag queen. She prowled the rooms, trying to get a feel for the woman.

From what she could gather at a cursory glance, no one else lived here. And there was nothing masculine anywhere, nothing to suggest Franny lived with a man. Birth control pills and tampons testified she wasn't one. But Skip would know a lot more after the crime lab had done its work.

Abasolo had just come with her for backup, and had a meeting scheduled. He left when the coroner arrived.

Alone, Skip took care of the mopping up. And when the crime lab was done, she assessed once more, now free to take in the details.

By now she already knew, from Franny's driver's license, that the victim's true name was Frances Reynaud, and that she did indeed live at this address.

Skip opened closets and drawers. All the clothes were women's, many with designer labels. There were no photos anywhere. Not much attention had been paid to the kitchen—oddly, there were cheap plates, but plenty of Waterford glasses. Clearly Franny was a person who entertained only for cocktails—or at least had done so once. Skip had the impression of someone who'd invite a friend over, realize she had no glasses, and go down to Adler's, buy out half the store, then hop over to Hurwitz-Mintz for an instant living room. The place looked as if Franny had bought things fast, without shopping much, just gathering things she thought she ought to have.

And that she could suddenly afford, Skip thought.

There were only a few books, mostly coffee table tomes about New Orleans, and one or two paperbacks. The paperbacks, curiously, were both about Marie Laveau, the Nineteenth Century Voodoo Queen. Skip was startled. She hadn't seen candles, an altar, anything except the cards to suggest an interest in the occult. A voodooist would have a much funkier house, littered with the bits and pieces of a complicated system of worship. So Franny probably hadn't been a devotee, and from the looks of her bookcase, she didn't care much for history, either. Still, many people, including Skip herself, were fascinated by Marie Laveau. She opened one of the books and began leafing through.

A drawing caught her eye, a picture of Marie fixing a white woman's hair, and she remembered that the priestess had also been a hairdresser, that it was said she was so good at divination because she already knew everyone's secrets. What woman doesn't talk to her hairdresser?

Turning the page, Skip saw that a paragraph to that effect had been highlighted. Her scalp started to prickle.

The opposite is true, too, she thought. If you're having your Tarot read, you probably tell more secrets than you're told.

It certainly gave Skip something to think about. Something that made her look around for a few household records. Sure enough, in the closet was a file box containing a file marked simply, "house." The deed had been filed there, along with copies of Franny's original offer, the seller's counteroffer, and the final contract. All the documents listed Franny as the buyer. If she had a sugar daddy, he'd given her cash.

But Skip was betting she didn't.

Next, she found an address book, which she leafed

through from A to Z. Curiously, she noted that most of the names were those of women.

She moved on to an appointment book and saw that Franny had had quite a few repeat clients. Three names—Roz Bordelon, Holly Mayfair, and Mona Spindel—appeared about once a month. Actually, looking more carefully, Spindel had stopped getting readings awhile ago, but had been back within the last week.

Skip checked the phone book. Uh-huh. There she was. Or rather, there *they* were—Charles and Mona, on Philip Street. That meant a husband, a nice home in the Garden District, and for Skip, an idea that was growing.

She was remembering something a psychiatrist, a particularly witty one, had once said to her at a cocktail party. "I keep hoping," he said, "that some day Hamlet's going to walk through that door. But no. It's always Othello—day after day after day."

"Relationship problems?" Skip had laughed, figuring he exaggerated, but perhaps psychiatry and the cards had a lot in common. It certainly suggested a way Franny could have come by the house with all its nice new Waterford.

Next, she found Franny's savings account book, and there, plain as day, was what she needed. No big deposits at all in the last week or so, in fact just a few bucks in the bank.

But plenty of deposits in the previous two years, plainly marked with the initials "MS". There were also past due bills—Franny had needed a new roof and hadn't had the wherewithal to pay for it.

Skip's hunch was growing so strong she was impatient to play it, but first she canvassed the neighbors and learned two or three had heard the shot, but thought it was something else. Better yet, one had noticed a woman visiting Franny two nights before.

Skip couldn't wait to get to Franny's colleagues on the Square. As it happened, Skip had friends on the psychic circuit, as did nearly everybody in the French Quarter, which is only about thirteen blocks in area. But what a thirteen blocks! Walker Percy said there were "more nuns and naked ladies" in New Orleans than anywhere else, but Skip was pretty sure he meant her neighborhood alone. The quarter had everything else as well, and Starlady, as it happened, lived around the corner from her.

The astrologer liked to get to the Square about midafternoon, usually after a visit to the library—she was hooked on detective fiction, and there was a lot of dead time between customers.

None of the regulars were at their tables except the self-proclaimed Goddess of Jackson Square, who was wearing peacock feathers today. Skip got a Lucky Dog and went down to the levee for a river break.

By the time she returned, Starlady was there, having indeed been to the library; she was poring over a Marcia Muller novel as if there were no tomorrow. She made her living, however, betting that there was, and routinely tapped into it via a thoroughly up-to-date astrology program installed in her laptop, which she kept at the ready in case a customer interrupted her reading.

Skip approached. "Good book?"

"Hey, Skip. Sit down and talk to me."

"You'll never get a customer that way."

"Oh, who needs one? I'm reading."

"Have you heard about Franny?"

Her lips arranged themselves into something Skip couldn't quite make out. "What happened?"

"Somebody shot her."

"Umph." The astrologer nodded her hugely hatted head,

seemingly waiting for details.

"You don't seem too surprised."

"Something about her—I don't know. Whoever heard of a psychic who takes checks?"

Skip laughed, as she supposed she was meant to. "Why? Because you know in advance they're going to bounce?"

"No, no—it's too commercial or something. I can't put my finger on it."

"You sound as if you think she was up to something."

"I guess I had a weird feeling about her." Starlady smiled and lifted an eyebrow. "She used to read at the Tea Leaf. Maybe they're like that there."

Skip supposed it was a psychic's privilege to be enigmatic. She bade farewell to her neighbor and made her way to the Tea Leaf Palace, an institution nearly as old as the Square itself (though the old-timers say they haven't always sold crystals there). It's a storefront equipped with booths for readers, some of whom have been there for years and enjoy a certain amount of local fame. If Franny had read there, she had worked among the elite of her ilk.

The woman at the counter wore flowing robes and a sequined scarf around a head of red curls, as if she'd stopped by a uniform store and picked up a gypsy suit. Skip stated her name and business. "I hear Franny used to work here," she began and waited a moment, but got no response. "I was wondering if you could tell me a little about her."

The woman's jaw tightened. "I don't know anything about it."

"I didn't mean the murder. It's Franny herself I'm interested in. What sort of clients she liked to see, what her specialty was—"

The gypsy laughed, a sort of bray that sprayed saliva. "Specialty! Honey, in this business, there's *no* such thing as a specialty. Only one question in the world. Client after client after client—they've only got one thing on their mind."

Bingo, Skip thought. Othello. "Relationships?" She asked.

"You'd think nobody in the world gave a damn for the stock market or ever got diagnosed with a fatal disease. It's love, love, love. Oh, well—" Skip restrained herself from completing the sentence with her: "Makes the world go 'round."

"And are any of these lovers already married?"

The woman brayed again. "Oh, all of 'em—to somebody else."

"Somehow I just had that feeling." Skip smiled. "I bet they're repeaters, too."

To her surprise, the gypsy returned her smile. "Repeat offenders, you'd probably call 'em."

"So Franny must have had a pretty regular clientele."

The gypsy got a peculiar look on her face. "Seemed to—but somebody sure didn't like her."

"The person who killed her, you mean."

"Oh." She turned pink, in sudden confusion. "No, I didn't mean that. I meant the person who got her fired."

Music, Skip thought, to my ears. She uttered only one pregnant syllable: "Oh?"

"Never did find out why. Just one day there was a call and then she was out of here."

"A call to whom?"

"The shop owner." She inclined her head toward a dapper man bent over a Tarot layout. "Joseph over there."

In a thick accent Skip couldn't identify, Joseph informed her that personnel matters were confidential and that she was at worst tacky, at best tactless for daring to bring up the subject.

"I gather," Skip said, "that you're not a citizen."

"You gather wrong."

"Evidently, you need filling in on the laws of the land. This is a murder case; I need your help. Do I make myself clear?" In fact, there wasn't much she could do if he didn't cooperate, but he crumbled fast. And the words he said were the ones she wanted to hear. Franny had been fired for blackmailing a customer: Mona Spindel.

Mona must have had a dalliance, confided the fact to her reader, and paid for the reading with a check, which gave Franny her name, address, and all-important phone number. After that, Mona had kept on paying—until she got tired of it and ratted Franny out.

But Franny had had bills to pay and made the mistake of messing with Mona again. Skip thought she would have done well to remember that Uptown ladies were famous for packing pistols. She headed for Philip Street.

By evening she had the weapon, an ID from the neighbor who'd seen Franny's visitor, and Mona in a cell.

A nice neat package, she thought—except for a loose end that threatened to drive her crazy. She went back to the square to demand answers.

Evening was Starlady's best time. She was reading by candlelight. "I've got a question," said Skip. "You didn't even seem rattled when I told you about Franny. How come you were so cool?"

"I expected it, of course. I did her chart a year ago."

"You're saying you predicted this?"

"Certainly. I warned her, in fact."

"Oh, come on."

"Ask anyone on the Square. Everyone knew it was coming." She gave Skip her raised eyebrow. "What do you think we are—a bunch of quacks?"

Too Mean to Die

LACEY

My mother is a husk now, the juice that fueled her drained away,
nothing in her that any of us recognizes. Her skin is not hers
either, falling in a thousand velvet folds around her neck,
stretched over a body so large her hips can barely fit through a
doorway. Her eyes are eerily quiet.

I remember when they flashed with malice and evil. You
could see the glint from clear across the room, quick and
mean and ready to strike. But she was not like a snake, in and
out, its ruin inflicted in less time than it takes a tongue to
flick. Wanda, as she is called, was more like some parody of a
kitten at the tit, the mother the sucking one, first inflicting the
wound, then biting it, lacerating, gnawing at it with fearsome,
sickening relish. For more than fifty years, she has tortured
my father in this fashion, scoring a thousand strikes a day,
chewing at her own venomous gashes.

We were not immune, Darlene and Will and me. To us,
mother love was more the knuckle sandwich than the home-
baked cookie. Baking, hah. She was about as likely to bake as
make us prom dresses.

What did she do instead? Oh, she had jobs; plenty of them,
one after another. She worked for the welfare, or in somebody's store, or, once, in a hospital. And she was always,
every single time, the only competent person, the only one
who had the least idea what they were doing in the entire

place. And every blessed time, the boss not only was unable to grasp this, he was so stupid that instead he favored her enemy, the one who for inexplicable reasons had taken a dislike to my mother and made it his or her business to destroy her. There was always one of these.

Even though these jobs made her life a torture beyond human experience, it was necessary that she do them because our father was so incompetent he couldn't even support his own family. He himself worked—it wasn't that he didn't, or that he couldn't keep his job—it was just that he always either gave away his money to some undeserving relative in distress or made some imbecile investment that my mother advised him against.

I was in sixth grade, I think, or maybe fifth, when Grandma stopped coming over after school. (Our parents had to pay her to take care of us, even though she was a relative, a fact that stuck deep in my mother's craw.) And so when Wanda judged I was old enough, I guess, she said, "Lacey, you're in charge now."

And I would have been if I could have gotten Darlene and Will to mind, which I couldn't. But I did learn to cook, or I was starting to, I was cooking some really good things, that Daddy and Will and Darlene were really enjoying, when Wanda got sick with that stomach thing. She couldn't eat anything but boiled vegetables and well-done meat, which I cooked separately for her for awhile, but she said it wasn't fair because she was always tempted to eat what everyone else was eating, and that made her sick. And being sick made her even meaner. So I had to stop cooking anything good.

Shortly before she told me I was in charge she stopped hitting me except for the occasional slap in the face. There had been a time when she delighted in fingering the back of a hairbrush, caressing the small trough in the middle, speculating aloud what it would feel like on my bare bottom, or Will's, what mark the groove would make. Will can remember it too, and neither of us knows why she stopped, though Darlene is five years younger than he, seven years younger than I—a more satisfying target, probably, and we glance nervously at her when we mention it. But I have asked her, and she insists she doesn't know what I'm talking about. I think it might be true.

It's possible she missed the worst times, the years we were poorest, perhaps. And she couldn't be expected to remember the years Wanda was maddest at our father for getting her pregnant again. When Darlene was little, Wanda whaled away on us.

But there are ways and ways of inflicting pain and I'd rather suffer a hundred brushes on my bottom than have my baby sister go through what Wanda did to her when she was just coming into her own. Darlene was always such a meek little thing. You had to notice—even if you were Wanda— how she came to life when she started singing and playing. Taking that away from her was the meanest thing our mother ever did. Darlene doesn't talk about it.

She's a little thick—always has been—but she's not a complete fool. Even she wouldn't mistake Wanda for Harriet Nelson. She's perfectly aware, along with the rest of us, of the change that's come over our mother.

The odd thing is that she is not the most upset of us. She always loved Wanda more, or so it seemed, probably because she believes she suffered less at her hands than the rest of us did. We are not one of those painfully repressed families in which things are simply Not Talked About. Our parents yelled constantly at each other, and at us. We yelled continuously at each other and our parents, despite the danger. We were expected to, I think. We were provoked. A disrespectful child could be punished, and there was joy in that—the delight of hurting someone for their own good, and because you knew you were right, and because they had wronged you.

Yes. Our parents called us names and we hurled insults right back at them, allowing invective to splatter like slime in the closeness and chaos of the tiny house. And later, when we had all got over it, when the poison had been worn and washed away by years and tears, we talked about it. Once, when Darlene was still in Winona, Wanda was hospitalized and Darlene said to me, "Don't worry, Lacey. You know she's too mean to die." Even Darlene. We never pretended.

So I knew things were bad when I read the medical records. "Mrs. Dewberry," the doctor wrote, "is a very pleasant eighty-one-year-old woman . . ."

Now what reason would he have for writing that if he didn't think it was true? And she couldn't fake it, it just isn't in her. Or didn't used to be. Because of the eyes; the meanness in the eyes. And a certain set of the lips. And a clipped way she had of speaking, especially to doctors, because she knew so much more than they did. A nasty, know-it-all quality. Pleasantness was not a thing she could fake.

I remembered some of the things our father had said—how docile she'd been about taking her medicine, how she wasn't complaining about the meals he got from the supermarket deli, how she tolerated his housekeeping.

She must be really weak, I thought; it must be close to the end.

So I took a big chance and let the sous-chef babysit the restaurant and went back to Winona for Thanksgiving. For a family pow-wow. The three of us had conferred by phone and decided to assess things.

It was unusual for us all to be there, though not so strange for the other two. Will lives in Jackson, which is so close he can't decently stay away, and Darlene, ever the dutiful, has always gone home when she can, though she can't get a minute's peace in her own hometown. Darlene grew up to be the biggest celebrity that ever came out of Winona and probably ever will. She started her singing in the Baptist church choir, a fact that nobody in town can forget for a second.

It had been six months—when Wanda had made the effort for our cousin Sara's wedding—since we'd last seen her, and in that short half-year the mother we knew had quietly left. Wanda lay in bed now twenty-four hours a day, hearing aids tucked into a drawer, TV at top volume, wispy hair to her shoulders, reeking of urine because she couldn't be bothered to have her diaper changed. She spoke only when spoken to, and then in monosyllables.

The odd thing, the thing no one could have predicted, was that we were all devastated.

Crushed.

Awash in sadness.

All four of us, though our father had probably felt that way for some time.

Darlene cried her heart out, but was no surprise. She wouldn't be the great songwriter and singer she is—and she's a giant, even to her sister—if she weren't sensitive.

As for Will, he was furious. At Wanda herself, at her doctors, at our father. Mad as a hornet.

I simply felt lost, like any kid wanting its mother. Wanda had always been there and now she wasn't. Wasn't dead, just wasn't there. Had turned into a cipher who refused to comb her hair, refused to get up, refused to eat, and all perfectly politely—she just wasn't interested.

But then she surprised us all and did get up. She came all the way down the hall on her walker while we were at dinner, wearing only her nightgown, hair still uncombed, diaper still reeking. She smiled as she hove into view, a triumphant smile, a nice smile, and I caught a glimpse of her eyes.

They were pretty.

They were soft; the eyes of a woman who'd made a big effort out of love.

They were not my mother's eyes.

And yet they were. I was aware, suddenly, of the soft side of her, the side she never showed, but that must have been there, as none of the three of us is currently in prison or a mental institution. Darlene was always aware of it, and Will may have been. I wasn't. For me, it had been better to be alert, not to expect a cookie when a knuckle sandwich was probably coming.

That funny little glimpse made me inexpressibly sad, revealing as it did a hidden reservoir, an unmistakable spark of vitality.

There was still somebody in there. But who?

Not the old Wanda. And yet, now and then, there were even signs of that. It used to be she'd buttonhole you and bend your ear and hold you hostage for hours while she assassinated someone's character. Now she barely grunts, and our father has succumbed to advanced loggorrhea to take up the slack. Still, we try. We take her little tidbits of news and offer them.

That Thanksgiving I went in to brush her hair, which is always all snarly these days except when the visiting nurse has just come. I sat on her bed and brushed and nattered on about Lucy Blaze, Darlene's little girl who raises rabbits and won't eat chicken or anything with ears. She will eat shellfish and oysters, because they're ugly, and fish because they have no fur, but she draws the line at chickens, though they are earless.

Wanda rallied for a moment. "Did y'all have to make her somethin' special for dinner?"

It was the straight line I was hoping for. "No, no problem," I said, already laughing. "She eats turkey because turkeys are stupid."

Such a funny little kid foible, the kind of thing that gives a grandma a giggle. Wanda didn't giggle. She said in so harsh a tone it was almost familiar: "Strange little girl, Lucy Blaze. Odd little creature." For a moment her eyes burned with the old danger, and I drew back, as always.

Out of the blue, she grabbed the brush and began grooming herself with a fury I thought had left her. When her arm stopped, she had left again.

She used to be a Christian. I am not one, but when I was growing up I was almost jealous of what she seemed to have. I felt she was onto something I didn't understand, and indeed she never lost an opportunity to inform me how barren her life would be without Jesus, how stupid I was for missing out on him.

Where is Jesus now, I wonder? For her life is a desert.

We all saw it, but Darlene reacted on a grand scale. That was the weekend she got the idea of dedicating a song to our mother on national television.

WANDA

They say I'm not dying. They say I'm at no greater risk than anyone else, those two little strokes could have happened to anyone. They prattle on about exercise and muscle atrophy and "depression" and "motivation" until I think I'll scream.

Well, no. I don't. I don't feel like screaming any more. Too much work; not worth it. I just want them to shut up. But I don't even care very much whether they do or they don't because I can read the supermarket ads in the paper or think about my soaps or count to a hundred or pretend I have to go to the bathroom. That's what I do when the visiting nurses come. I go to the bathroom so I don't have to listen to them.

They wanted me to get my hair cut because my family was coming. They wanted me to be able to get up and take a bath and get dressed and go to the table. I couldn't see why I should bother. I told them I would practice walking to-morrow. They said, no, I wasn't going to get away with that one again, but I didn't know what they meant. I thought I might feel better tomorrow.

Thomas asks me every Sunday if I want to go to church, and when I think of church I get a feeling, a kind of peaceful feeling, for a second or so. But it swims away so fast I'm not sure what it is. It doesn't seem worth the two hours it would take to get up and bathe and dress.

I don't know if I need that feeling, or any other feeling. The world seems gray most of the time. Colorless and neu-tral.

Comfortable.

Why can't they get this?

Why don't the nurses leave me alone? And Thomas and Lacey? All of them. They ask me how I feel and I say that I'm comfortable. Why is that not enough? When I pee, I like to sit in the warmth. That is comfortable. Changing my clothes is not.

I told Will that and a look of such disgust came over his face that I felt . . . I don't know what I felt. The grayness stopped for a second and turned a color. But I don't know what color. It wasn't bad, it was kind of good.

Something is bad, though.

Something is.

This is why I have to have my medicine, especially my Restoril, for sleep. I can say it—I think I can say it. There is something very, very bad. Like monsters. But *not* monsters.

There is something. I don't know where it is or what it is, but there *is* something.

I try to think what it is, but then it swims away.

And there's something else too, something maybe not bad. Not frightening anyway. Sometimes, for just a flicker, I feel . . . alive. Like my old self.

Thomas says I play games with the nurses, even with the children, that I lie to them about "tomorrow". But I don't. It is not a game or a lie, because I feel this flicker now and then. The trouble is that no one will help me. They talk, but they don't really talk. They act as if I'm already dead.

Lacey, for instance. Well, Lacey's always been Miss Condescending Priss, better than anyone in *this* house. Lacey came in at Thanksgiving and started to talk about Lucy Blaze, that out-of-control brat of Darlene's. I don't know what's wrong with Darlene, letting the child run wild like that. Blue hair. Two holes in one ear, three in the other. God knows how many in her navel.

Well, Lacey came in to brush my hair and started to talk about her. I thought she was going to ask me about her, to ask my opinion about what's to be done . . . and just for a minute, I felt the flash, the flicker—like a little burst of energy. I must have felt needed. And then Miss Lacey-Pants clammed up on me.

I don't know why, but I grabbed the brush and attacked my own hair. That brush felt good in my hand, too. Familiar, kind of, like an old friend.

Will is the same as Lacey. He came in to talk about that TV thing Darlene's gotten herself so puffed up about. And I *know* she's going to fall flat on her face. I know how far in over

101

her head she is with that one—I'm still her mama. But I tried to talk to him about it—I thought maybe we could do something before she embarrasses herself in front of God and everybody, but he just said, "Oh, I don't think there's anything to worry about." Brushing me off. Like I'm already dead.

And Darlene. She doesn't even try. She's been holding a grudge since she was fourteen.

DARLENE

Mama was the one who gave me music. The Baptist Church had a children's choir for which you didn't have to have talent, you just had to show up. It was the last thing I was interested in.

My sister Lacey was my after-school babysitter in those days, but she had French Club on Thursdays. Mama made me join the choir because they had practice that day, so I'd have a place to go.

Fuss! You should have seen me. I yelled and screamed for an hour the night before the first time, I don't know why. It's not like I had anything more important to do than play jacks.

The first time it wasn't much. The second time I started to get the hang of it. In three months, when I figured out what was going on, I had my heart set on singing the solo on Easter Sunday. Mama didn't think I was ready, so I said "yes ma'am" all nice and sweet and begged and begged to take piano lessons, thinking she might trade out one for another. She wouldn't, though. She said we couldn't afford it.

I did the solo the next year, and that was the first time I really understood what an audience was like, but that wasn't the main thing. The main thing was the music. I can't explain it, but it made me feel different from anything else—made me feel like *me*.

In those days, when the three of us ran wild like little

heathens in the afternoons, Will and I used to listen to the country station, which Mama would never have let us do if she'd known. He had a friend, Sammy Lee Turner, who'd come over and bring his guitar in the afternoons, and sometimes I'd pick it up and play with it. Sammy Lee taught me some chords and things, and then I just started messing around, and I kind of figured out how to play it by myself.

I asked for my own guitar for Christmas, but Mama said it would cost too much, so I hired myself out cleaning houses. I wasn't but ten years old.

I knew how to clean, though, and in no time I had me a lucrative clientele. But old Miz Woodhouse bragged on me to Mama at church one day, and that was the end of that. Mama didn't know I was doing it, see. She said she'd never been so embarrassed in all her life. Her daughter, cleaning houses. Humph! She said if I needed money so bad why didn't I ask for it, and I said I had asked for a guitar and she said we couldn't afford it. I don't think she liked that too much, but Daddy laughed and said, "Oh, hell. I'll buy you the damn guitar." And he did.

I was still listening to my favorite country station, singing along with Emmy Lou and Dolly and Loretta, and also still singing in the choir when I was about fourteen. Lacey was gone by then and Will might as well have been, with football and all. I'd come home every afternoon and be there all by myself. It wasn't a good time for me, without Lacey and Will.

Mama and Daddy were fighting a lot in those days, and Daddy was drinking too. That's when I started writing.

I spent my afternoons that way, playing the guitar and writing songs and mooning around listening to the radio.

My first song was about leaving Winona and going to Nashville, can you feature that? Even then I was thinkin' about it. And there was this talent show right on the station I listened to every day of my life. I played the song for my friend Rosalie Ansell and she made me enter. She said I had to, I really had talent, nobody else she knew could do that. At first, I said I couldn't because the station was too far away, and she up and volunteered to give me a ride to Memphis. Just like that. (Or rather, she said she'd get her brother Jimmy to drive us, Jimmy being sixteen and having a license.) She said we'd get up a bunch of us to go. We'd spend Friday night in the Admiral Benbow, then we'd get up Saturday morning and go on over and I'd win the talent contest.

In our imagination, we had a whole car-full—Rosalie and me and Jimmy and Jimmy's friend, Larry, who Rosalie had a crush on, and a fat guy named Bobby who was a friend of Jimmy and Larry's. We weren't really going to do it, of course. It was just talk. I was just going to go over and spend the night with Rosalie and we were going to laugh about what if we did do it.

What I didn't know was that Rosalie's parents were out and she'd already written a note saying she was spending the night at my house. Well, I wasn't about to go along with that. Uh-uh. I knew I was going to get my hide tanned if I got caught. Rosalie said, don't be silly, the worst that would happen was we'd all get grounded for a while. I wouldn't have done it, either, if I hadn't wanted to win that contest so bad.

I wonder what made me think I could win it? That Saturday morning I was so exhausted I could hardly pick up a guitar. I'd spent the night lying in a bed with Rosalie at the Benbow Inn, while the three boys slept on the floor at our feet. And Jimmy Ansell was *cute,* did I mention that? The whole situation was so strange I didn't sleep a wink, but it must have been good for my singing. Because I did win.

Everything would have been fine if Will hadn't been listening to the radio that morning.

Mama heard me singing and there was hell to pay. It didn't even wait till we got back to Winona to start. Three deputies picked us all up at the radio station, and arrested the boys for transporting minors or something. No matter how many times we told them the boys slept on the floor, it wasn't good enough.

But the upshot was, they let the boys go, and all the others got grounded for a few weeks, just like Rosalie said.

That wasn't what happened to me. Mama grabbed me by the arm and her eyes were like cold blue fire. "You little idiot!" she said. "You little fool! You have humiliated me so bad I can never hold my head up in this town again. What am I going to do with you?"

I held my breath, knowing it wasn't going to be anything good. "First of all," she said, "you are going to quit the choir. You have sung with that choir your last time."

"Oh, Mama, no!" I hollered. I couldn't believe she'd do that to me.

"Yes, ma'am. Absolutely. And *then,* you are gon' quit the glee club. You have sung with the glee club your last time."

"You don't mean that," I said. I really didn't think she did.

"And *then,* she said, "you are gon' bring me all the radios in the house."

I just stared at her, having no idea what that was about.

"Do it!" she hollered, and I did it.

She put them all in a pile. "That's for the Goodwill," she said, and sure enough, she took them there the next day.

"Now go get me your guitar," she said.

"Mama, no!" I screamed, and she went and got Daddy's belt.

"Get it by the count of five. One . . . two . . ." like I was five years old.

But I didn't know what else to do but get it, so I did and when I came back she was holding Daddy's hammer.

She said, "Now you take this and go out in the back yard and smash it up."

I said, "No, Ma'am, I can't do that," and she tried to pull me, but I just dug in my feet and wouldn't go.

And then she put the guitar right on the kitchen table and she got that blue fire look in her eyes again, and she said, "Do you understand what you did to me, Darlene? I have never been so embarrassed in all my life."

She raised the hammer and smashed my guitar, and I sat down on the kitchen floor and screamed. Then she did it again; kept right on doing it until her arm got tired, I guess, or until she got tired of hearin' me scream.

I can't explain it, I felt like she was killing that guitar, even though I knew it was never alive. I felt as if I had a friend who just got murdered. I spent the next year lying on my back in bed, cryin'.

But I bounced back just fine. I'm sure I deserved it, anyway. After all, what fourteen-year-old girl has the right to lie to her parents and take off for another state with three boys? Mama was just doing what she thought was right, underscoring a point so I'd be sure and get it.

I can laugh about it now—last year I was named Favorite Female Country Artist, and that woman is the one who gave me music in the first place. If she hadn't taken it away, I might never have known how to appreciate it. I might not have even made it to Nashville.

I owe Mama a lot, and it just broke my heart to see her the way she was the Thanksgiving before my TV special. I wanted to cheer her up so *bad*. I wanted my mama back. Until the last year or so, she was always such a stage mother—real, real proud of her little girl who made it after her mama started her off in the Baptist Church choir. And she was a real good Christian. She used to talk about it all the time we were growing up—how important Jesus was in her life, how she couldn't get along without him—you'd have thought he was a real person. You know that hymn about the garden? "He walks with me and he talks with me and he tells me I am his own"? You know, like they're lovers or something? That's her favorite.

I was casting about for some way to make her feel better when I got this great idea I could sing it for her on my special. Of course I really couldn't—too Jesus-y, I guess—but I realized I *sure* could do "Amazing Grace." In fact, I thought, why not dedicate the whole damn show to her?

Lacey was so mean about it you wouldn't believe it. You know what she said? What she actually had the nerve to say? She said, "Darlene, do you really think she'd appreciate it?"

I said, "Well, she's not dead, you know. Just a little out of it."

And then, the oddest thing. Lacey got all misty all of a sudden. She said, "She's never never never going to be anybody other than who she is."

I didn't have the slightest idea what the hell she was talking about, especially since Mama already was somebody different from who she is, and Lacey and I had talked about it, which I reminded her of.

She gave me a little half-smile. "All I mean is, don't expect a response from her."

I said, "I'm just trying to cheer her up—what's so wrong with that?"

Lacey said, "You can't buy love, Darlene," and I finally got it. My sister's a jealous bitch sometimes; and besides she's never gotten along with Mama. Her problems just aren't my problems.

It got closer and closer to the special and Mama got more and more withdrawn, more and more into her soaps, more reluctant to talk as time went on. At least that's what Daddy said. But he kept saying she was up to coming and being in the audience, and so did all her doctors. So we flew her there, along with Daddy and two nurses.

I got them a real nice suite at the Four Seasons and sent Mama a blue dress that matched her eyes, plus a hairdresser and make-up expert, so she could be pampered in the comfort of her king-sized hotel bed.

She looked beautiful the night of the show. She was in the audience for awhile, so the camera could light on her every once in awhile, and then they brought her backstage for the finale, which was "Amazing Grace" preceded by a little speech I gave about how I owed my music to my mama, almost the same story I just told. Well, I broke down when I gave it. Right there on national television.

Well, finally I got it together enough to sing, and I sang, and that live audience went crazy. And then the credits rolled and they brought Mama onstage in her wheelchair and everything, and I leaned over and instead of hugging me, she hugged my guitar, which I was still wearing around my neck.

I didn't know what to think. Mama's not exactly right, but she does know her own daughter from a guitar.

"Mama, let go," I said, and I stayed where I was because I couldn't straighten up. But she didn't let go and I felt her looking at me, trying to tell me something, maybe. I looked right into her eyes, which were about three inches from mine. I knew I'd seen that look before. I couldn't place it right away, but it made me feel bad. Real bad. "Mama, what is it?" I said, leaning forward so it would just look like I was kissing her on the cheek, and she kicked me. Kicked me! Right on national television.

I was so shocked I jerked myself up, but Mama still held onto the guitar. The strap around my neck broke, and she ended up holding that guitar so tight you'd have thought it was a baby. She had a funny look on her face, like that was what she wanted all the time, and finally she spoke to me. She said, "I have never been so embarrassed in my whole life," and her eyes were like cold blue fire.

Now put that together, why don't you. I know I sure can't. All I know is, my feelings were so hurt I ended up cryin' in bed for six months, just like that other time.

I tried to talk to Mama about it, but she talks less than ever these days—just lies there and watches those everlastin' soaps.

But Lacey; *she'll* talk about it. She shakes her head and says I should have known. But how could I have known? How? If I live to be a hundred, I'll never figure it out.

Montezuma's Other Revenge

"McDonald, meet me at Perry's in an hour, okay?"

I stared at my computer, unable to imagine what was going to fill up the next three chapters of my current master-work—I already had two chases and a brawl. And as my answering machine burbled on, I was also unable to imagine the arrogance of someone who expected me to drop this wildly important project at the snap of his larcenous fingers.

"I've got a job for you—same as last time, $55 an hour."

Sixty, I thought, on account of the short notice.

"I've been burgled."

Suddenly the disembodied voice had my full attention. This was like a man biting a dog. Or kidding a kidder, maybe. The speaker was Booker Kessler, my very good friend—the burglar from the right side of the tracks who planned to stop burgling as soon as his psychoanalysis started working out. Booker could probably have gotten into Fort Knox if he put his mind to it. He was the quintessential second story man, the pro of pros, the consummate criminal. If he'd been burgled, I could be at Perry's in forty-five minutes. This was one story I wanted to hear.

And then of course there was the matter of the money. Though I am a mystery writer by trade, the popular acclaim I deserve continues to elude me and so, therefore, do the bucks I need.

Booker was already at Perry's, sipping a Perrier. I bellied up, and said, "So who'd burgle a burglar?" followed by, "I'll have a gin and tonic, please."

"Well, actually, I just said that to get you interested."

"You mean you weren't burgled? I'm going to pick up my toys and go home."

"Well, I think I was. Technically. I mean, I'm not sure. But it wasn't breaking and entering. I let the thief in of my own free will, and spent the afternoon pleasing and delighting her beyond all human imagining."

"Ungrateful wench." I tried not to laugh, but apparently not hard enough. I ended up spewing gin all over the bar.

"I met her at the Billboard Cafe," Booker said with dignity. He shrugged, as if to say, what's a fellow to do? "She just walked up to my table. I was with another woman too. She said she'd seen me around and always wanted to meet me and thought she'd introduce herself. So I asked her to join us. And then Kristi had to go back to work . . ."

"Hold it. She just walked up to your table? Weren't you a tiny bit suspicious?"

He shrugged. "Hell, no. They do that all the time."

I held my head. "Okay. She introduced herself. What's her name?"

"CeeCee."

"Um. Name-damaged. CeeCee what?"

Once again he shrugged, not succeeding even slightly in his pathetic effort to be the most nonchalant guy on Union Street. "I don't know, McDonald. There wasn't any reason to ask."

"For your sake, Booker, I hope you practice safe sex."

"Jealous?"

"Okay. So you and CeeCee ended up at your place—"

"Where she admired the artworks. One in particular—and after she left I realized it was missing."

"Oh, no!" For the first time I was genuinely sympathetic.

Booker has spent his ill-gotten gains on a truly fabulous art collection—mostly paintings, but some sculptures—of which he's justly proud.

"Actually, it wasn't anything that special. I mean, it's a pretty good piece, but I'd only had it a day or two and hadn't fallen in love yet."

"What was it?"

"A sculpture—a ceramic piece, actually—by a Central American artist who signs his work 'Miguel.' He's just starting to catch on in this country. I know this sounds weird, but he works in a sort of Precolumbian style."

"You're right. It sounds weird."

"Well, he doesn't copy the pieces, but he's inspired by them—he takes off from them, combines designs, sort of. The piece I lost was kind of a little squatting toad that also looked a little like a crocodile. About so high." He held his hands six inches apart. "And CeeCee had one of those over-sized purses."

"What color?"

"Plain terra cotta."

"And what does CeeCee look like?"

"Oh, about five-four, a hundred and five pounds. Last seen wearing a black leather mini. Hair black for the first couple of inches—at the roots that is—and white for the next eight or ten. Sticks out about a foot. Berry-colored lips. And a lot of black stuff on the eyes."

"Every second female south of Market answers that description."

"As it happens, I do know something about her. She works at the Clay Gallery—where I purchased the sculpture."

And so at noon the next day—galleries never seem to open before lunchtime—I sauntered into the Clay Gallery (which wasn't on Clay Street, but South of Market) and asked to see

CeeCee, which is hard to say. CeeCee, it seemed, had taken the day off to pack.

"Pack?" said I, wondering if she were skipping town, and if she were, how many hours work I could get out of a cross-country chase.

"She got a one-woman show in L.A."

"Ah. She's an artist too."

The person I was talking to could have been CeeCee herself except that her hair was blue instead of white and hung to her right shoulder, yet grew only half an inch long above her left ear, which was pierced six times and harbored six earrings. Dawn, her name was.

"She's a ceramicist," said Dawn, indicating a particolored amoeba-like object about half my height and at least my weight. And I am not considered a small man.

"That's hers? I mean, she had a lot of those to pack?"

"She may take the whole week off," said Dawn.

I leaned closer, aping a smitten collector. A tiny placard said the artist was Cynthia C. Hollander. It was a start.

There was a C.C. Hollander on a small Potrero Hill street, and I figured that had to be my woman—or close enough. If she wasn't the right CeeCee, this one probably got enough of her calls to know where to find her. I headed over there.

Hers was a downstairs apartment, up a short flight of steps to a little porch. On the porch were some shards, as if a ceramicist, in her haste to get ready for her big one-woman show, had dropped a piece of her work. And yet these were plain terra cotta, not glazed as CeeCee's other piece had been. There was mail in the mailbox. No one answered the bell. I couldn't see in from the porch but there was a big uncurtained window that looked out on the street.

So of course I climbed down, found a few bricks to stand on, held onto the windowsill, and risked arrest by hoisting myself up high enough to see in. The place had been tossed, and thoroughly. The kind of tossed where they rip the upholstery to shreds.

I tried the door, which didn't open at first, but Booker had taught me the credit card trick. In ten minutes—Booker could have done it in 30 seconds—I had the door open. And by the stink I knew someone was dead.

CeeCee was under the sofa cushions, still wearing the black leather mini. Her throat had been slit.

In my reporting days I saw a lot of bodies, but I'd never seen this particular brand of mutilation and I felt my gorge rising in a manner unbecoming even to a part-time detective. That wasn't all. Sweat broke out on my forehead and my head felt light and swimmy.

I'm not the sort who faints—the job description precludes it—but if I were I couldn't have done it in peace because of the hideous noise that suddenly assailed my ears. I realized the burglar alarm had gone off with me standing over a body in a place which I had just broken into and entered. I heard sirens too. Or I thought I did until I shook my head once or twice to clear it.

At about that time, the telephone—which wasn't a burglar alarm at all—stopped ringing and a voice that said it was CeeCee's spoke to the caller. And then another female voice said, "Hi, CeeCee, it's just Mom calling. Good news, I think. Dad double-checked and it turns out we *could* cash out a bond and lend you the money for the packing and shipping charges. At least I think it'll cover them. It might help anyway. Give me a call when you get in."

As CeeCee's mom talked to her ex-daughter, I took great gulps of air, not caring what it smelled like, just needing to get it into my lungs. On some weird kind of automatic pilot, not knowing why, I followed the voice to its origin, an answering machine in a bedroom in roughly the same condition as the living room.

I took a minute there to pull myself together and then I went over the whole place. Apparently, there was another occupant—a female roommate who had the second bedroom. Her room hadn't been spared either. Nor had the bathroom and kitchen. And that was it—no studio, so I gathered CeeCee had one elsewhere.

I went back to her room to call the cops, and on a whim played back her messages. There were others from her mother, one from Dawn at the gallery, a couple from a wimpy-sounding guy named Jeremy, and two that caught my attention.

"It's Rico, Baby," said a whispery, nasty, smug, self-satisfied voice. "We've got Sabina. She'd make a real nice sacrifice and it just happens we could use one right now. Or maybe if you return my property we could find a cat or a chicken."

The second was also from Rico. It came after one Jeremy and two Moms, so probably a reasonable amount of time had elapsed in the interim. "Hi, Babe. The Aztecs would have loved this. Sabina's on the altar already, and I've got this really sharp knife—"

CeeCee picked up the phone at this point, sounding out of breath, "Rico? Rico, I just got in. And guess what, I made a big discovery. I dropped the sculpture, jerkoff.

"So now I'll set the terms, okay? Bring Sabina home now. And also bring $5000 . . ." Here, the machine clicked off, having recorded for as long as it was programmed to record.

But I got the idea. Dropping the statue had given CeeCee a whole new outlook on things—apparently because it contained information she could use for blackmail.

There was only one Rico—Rico Rainey—in CeeCee's

115

Rolodex. His address was a place called the Hall of Montezuma, on Minna Street.

I phoned Booker and quickly filled him in. When he was
breathing regularly again, I said, "Listen, I'm calling Blick
now. If I stay and tell him all this, it'll be at least a half hour,
maybe an hour and a half, before the cops make a move.

"Sabina must be the roommate. Maybe she's dead already
and maybe she's not, but I've been in a house with a corpse
and her mother's voice and some other stuff for 20 minutes
and I don't feel like waiting for Blick to get here and find out.
You want to meet me at the Hall of Montezuma, whatever
that may be, in ten minutes?"

"Yeah." His voice came out like a croak—he was shaken
by CeeCee's death.

Next I called my least favorite cop, Homicide Inspector
Howard Blick. "I want to report a homicide—"

"Who is this?"

"Jean-Paul Sartre. That's J-e- . . ."

"Spell it!"

"I'm trying to. J-e- . . ."

"G-e-what?"

Too late I realized it was going to take the whole ten minutes I had just to get the name spelled properly. If Blick had
become a tubewinder instead of a cop, the San Francisco Police Department would have been better served.

"Forget it," I said, and gave the address.

Back in the light of day, everything seemed very vivid, very
bright, and somewhat larger than life, which I felt damned
glad to be living at the moment. Details caught my eye—a
single rose blooming in CeeCee's tiny front yard, or front
flower bed—actually, just a strip of dirt; a ticket on a car
parked illegally across the street; Ceecee's handwriting on a
letter in her mailbox . . .

I investigated. Yes, the same writing on the Rolodex cards, and the return address was none other than her own—she'd sent herself a letter. I pulled it out and felt it. Heavy. I ripped it open—a locker key to God knew where. I put it in my pocket.

Booker was waiting for me, in jeans and a black leather jacket that had probably cost slightly less than I'd get for the book I was working on. His car was parked in front of the Hall, as unprepossessing a place as everything else on Minna Street. You found it by its label next to the buzzer—"Montezuma," a second floor hall. The door was unlocked.

Booker shrugged. "Do we go in?"

I nodded. "Sure. If anyone asks, we'll say we took a wrong turn on the way to the shores of Tripoli."

The stairs led to a loft—a much more hall-like space than I'd thought we'd find. A couple of torches burned on either side of the thing Rico must have meant when he spoke of the altar—though no maiden was currently being sacrificed on it. In fact, there was a caged chicken on it. The odor of incense hung thick in the air.

The place had no windows, but the walls were white, newly painted, and hung with Precolumbian masks that showed up well in the torchlight. Statues—also Precolumbian, or maybe fakes or Miguels—stood on pedestals that lined the walls. A bunch of them had been massed around the altar.

On the floor were small rugs, and some kind of weird music was playing. The whole effect wasn't so much eerie as trying way too hard for eerie and ending up bogus.

The thing that most spoiled the effect, to tell you the truth, was the table at the top of the stairs with a box marked "Donations" on it and the woman who sat behind it, her short, spiky magenta hairdo looking as if it would be wrecked beyond repair by an Aztec headdress.

"Hi," she said. "I'm Sabina."

Booker and I looked at each other, then quickly cased the Hall. Empty—or so it seemed, anyhow. I turned back to Sabina, put my face close to hers, smiled, and spoke very low. "Hi," I said. "CeeCee's dead."

Her eyes were blue, I noticed, as they expanded to resemble blue Frisbees, full of fear. Her jaw loosened and fell; I thought for a minute she was going to scream. She didn't, but she glanced around, terrified, as if she were surrounded. If it was an act, it was a good one.

I took her wrist. "Come on. We'll get you out of here."

She didn't even stop to grab her purse. She wasn't the soul of discretion, either. She had on those black, lace-up old-lady shoes that hip young ladies love so much and that have little heels on them that sound like a parade. She set her legs going like two blades of an egg beater, a woman pursued by demons on uncarpeted stairs, and there wasn't a thing we could do to stop her. We simply tore after her and once outside, slammed ourselves into Booker's car, peeling out like characters in an Eddie Murphy movie.

She was sitting on my lap in the front seat, since no one had time for the back, and she was crying now. Suddenly she caught on that she had leaped extremely precipitately into the arms of strangers. "Omigod!" she wailed. "Who are you?"

I didn't know where to start, but Booker said, "Are you CeeCee's roommate?"

She nodded.

"I'm the guy that bought the sculpture."

That seemed to satisfy her.

"We went looking for it," I said, "and found her."

Booker headed for Hamburger Mary's, and on the way we made a deal—our half of the story for Sabina's half.

118

Bucked up by a few beers, into which she would have been crying if such a thing were possible without making a spectacle of oneself, she explained first about the Hall of Montezuma.

"It's a cult, I guess you'd call it. I mean, Rico says it's a revival of the Aztec religion—they have all these weird rituals and chicken sacrifices. I don't know—they get a pretty good crowd some nights. Students go in for that sort of thing, you know, and some from the Art Institute went a few times and word got out about the artworks."

She paused for a minute, looking puzzled. "They aren't Aztec is the only thing—and a lot of them aren't really Precolumbian. But, anyhow, most of them are pretty good. So people started going to see them like it was a gallery. The rituals were like this added attraction or something. Anyhow, that's how CeeCee and I found the place."

"So who's Rico?"

"Rico? He's—uh—the priest, I guess you'd call it. He's—um—really handsome and kind of scary, like when he slits the chickens' throats, you know what I mean?"

We nodded.

"I don't know, that turns some people on, I guess. I mean, he has these women all over him all the time. CeeCee was one of them. He came around our place a lot."

She lowered her gaze, for a moment actually affording the tears a beer target. "He started coming on to me and, I don't know, I guess I was just competitive with CeeCee. I started seeing him over at the Hall. And then I kind of got hooked on him." She looked up again, the hard part over.

"What happened was, CeeCee got this big opportunity down in L.A.—I mean, it really is a big deal—it could make her a lot of money. But have you seen that elephantine stuff of hers? It was going to cost a fortune to get it there. So she asked Rico to lend her some money and he wouldn't do it. She asked him, see, because she knew how much goes into that Hall—it costs fifteen bucks to come to a ritual and then they always collect more money once you're there and everything. I mean, it really is a cult, although—" She stopped, as if trying to collect her thoughts.

"Although what?" I prompted.

"Something about Rico—he founded the thing and he's the high priest and everything, but he doesn't really talk about it when he's, like, off duty. Anyway, a lot of money comes through there, but the bastard wouldn't lend her any. He said it belonged to the church and he couldn't.

"Well, that pissed CeeCee off and I guess she was a little desperate, anyhow, so she took one of the statues. It wasn't hard because she sometimes worked the desk, like I was doing today, and I guess she thought he wouldn't notice. Anyway, she knew perfectly well what she could get for a Miguel at the gallery where she worked. To tell you the truth, she also knew they wouldn't ask a lot of questions about where she got it. Everything's on consignment, of course, but if someone bought it, she'd get just about enough to cover her expenses. And they have a list of preferred customers who'd been looking for something of the sort. They'd just arrange a private sale, the customer would never know the statue was stolen, and everybody'd be happy."

"Call me Mr. Preferred," said Booker.

Sabina nodded. "So it was sold almost the minute she stole it. But meanwhile I didn't know anything about any of this. I mean, I knew he hadn't lent her the money, but I didn't know she'd stolen something from him. So the way he told it, it got me all outraged, like how dare she? And he asked me to stay at the Hall a day or two and pretend to be kidnapped." She shrugged.

"So I said okay. Look, I was jealous. I'm an artist too and she was the one with the big break and everything—" Booker waved a hand, explaining that she didn't have to explain.

"Anyway, that was the last I heard. I didn't know she'd gotten it back—he didn't tell me—all's he said was he hadn't heard from her." Her eyes got big again. "And then he started talking about how that statue had a curse on it. I mean, it's not even *old*. And he said he was worried about her and all—"

I said, "You were getting suspicious, weren't you?"

She nodded, miserable. "I was really getting scared." Her voice was tiny.

"With good reason. When she tried to blackmail him, he apparently didn't waste any time."

She turned Frisbee eyes on me. "Would he have killed me too?"

"Maybe." Actually, I didn't think he would have, because he hadn't yet, but I needed her help and I wanted her mad as hell.

The plan we proceeded to put together was simple, and the first part went beautifully. That was the part where Sabina phoned Rico, said she had what was in the sculpture, or anyway, the key to it, that she'd be glad to give it to him for a small finder's fee—say $1,000 or so—and would he meet her later?

The next part went okay too. That was the part where we got Sabina some handcuffs and a gun. Booker knew someone who got the cuffs for us, but the gun, to tell you the truth, was one of those really realistic-looking squirt guns. However, it was going to be dark and Sabina wouldn't be alone.

The third part was the actual confrontation, due to occur at 7 p.m. in a very narrow alley near China Basin. We'd blocked one end with my car and the other with Booker's, so no one could drive in. If Rico came alone, we could take him;

if he didn't, Sabina would have time to get away in one of the cars.

At seven sharp, she stood between the cars, more or less in front of two one-story buildings across from each other. Booker was on top of one building, I was on top of the other. A man entered the alley—alone.

"Rico?" called Sabina.

"Yeah."

He kept coming till he'd passed Booker's car, had gotten about ten feet away from her. She was holding the gun with two hands, like the cops do on TV. It looked pretty real.

Sabina shouted, "Don't come any closer." Rico stopped.

"Empty your pockets."

While he did this was the perfect time to jump him, but we'd agreed we wouldn't do it till we were sure he wasn't armed. He threw a packet of bills at Sabina. She threw the locker key at him.

Cautiously, Rico knelt to pick it up. The moment had arrived. The plan was for me, being far the larger, to jump him and subdue him, Sabina helping with firearm threats. If there was real trouble, Booker would further surprise Rico by jumping on his head. Otherwise, he'd stay put till Sabina had produced the cuffs and then he'd come down and cuff Rico while I sat on him or something.

The only problem was, I slipped as I was starting to jump. I regained my balance, but Rico had caught on by this time, and he moved quickly. So did Sabina. And so, alas, did Booker. He meant to jump on Rico to take up the slack, but unfortunately, he landed on Sabina. She hollered, they both went down, it was general bedlam, and Rico took off running.

I jumped now, landing more or less safely (at any rate not breaking anything) and took off after him. He ran another block down our alley, then turned down a main street, and into another alley. I wasn't even close to catching him, but eventually he had to run out of steam. Or I did. In this neighborhood—industrial by day, deserted at night—we could probably trot about for hours unmolested. It was just a question of endurance. And I was panting like a Husky in hell.

I ran on, following the far distant footsteps, vaguely aware of some noise far behind me, blood pounding in my ears. And suddenly I realized Rico's footsteps had stopped. But too late. "Slow down, bro'," said a voice.

I not only slowed, I stopped. Two guys who looked burnt out—one white, one Chicano—had headed Rico off and captured him. That would have been great except that they didn't seem to be planning to turn him over to me. One was holding him by his collar, a knife at his throat. The other also had a knife. He took a step towards me.

And then I became better aware of the clatter behind me. About a milli-second later a female voice said, "Police. Freeze or I'll blow your heads off."

We all froze. The burnouts dropped their knives. And then Rico shouted, "Sabina!" and unfroze. He headed towards me, trying to get past. Now I really did jump him.

And a male voice said, "Police. Freeze or I'll blow your heads off."

It was one of the goddam muggers. Both of them were cops on some kind of surveillance job involving drugs, but we found out that part quite a bit later.

You'd think Blick would have been so grateful he'd have practically kissed my hand, but instead he made us stay at the Hall all night (Hall of Justice, not Montezuma), telling and retelling our stories, and not giving us anything back in return.

It all came out later, though. We had unwittingly, it

seemed, cracked a major gang of art thieves. That is, CeeCee had. The key opened a locker in the Greyhound terminal that held a small Precolumbian gold pendant. CeeCee had apparently dropped the Miguel and realized when the pendant fell out what Rico was up to, which was buying legitimate artworks and bringing them through customs filled with much more valuable stolen ones—part of a cache taken from a museum a few years ago. She'd stashed the pendant in the locker and mailed the key to herself, in case Rico tried to get tough—but she'd underestimated how tough he was going to get.

The pieces were being brought in slowly, one by one, at customs stations that didn't tend to X-ray. They were sold to well-heeled buyers out of Rico's storefront pseudo-Aztec cult, which made a nice cover. He didn't really need it, but he liked the drama, power, and extra bucks he got out of it. He had a record as long as a fishing line.

Incidentally, there was a reward involved—from the museum that lost the loot. Booker wasn't eligible, having melted into the shadows during the alley confrontation in which the "P" word was mentioned, but Sabina and I would have happily split it. That is, we would have if Blick hadn't explained about the 19 or 20 things he would charge us with if we tried to claim it.

He and the two undercover gorillas got it, a turn of events I blame on the ghost of a certain well-known Aztec emperor. After all, Booker and Sabina and I were the second bunch of gringoes to come along and demolish the Aztec religion.

Project Mushroom

It was June 29, the day before the end of the fiscal year, and Carla looked awful. She was trying to cheer herself up with a puny little joke. "We've decided to kill Martin," she said. "Everyone in the office is going to strike a blow, like in that Agatha Christie novel. Do we count you in or not?"

I shook my head. "I guess I haven't been here long enough. I'm nowhere close to murder."

"Just wait. He gets to everybody."

In fact, I'd been on Project Mushroom only about a week. The project's purpose was to figure out ways to increase California's mushroom sales income by several zillion bucks. It was funded by the State and administered by the State Department of Food and Agriculture, and if it wanted to continue being funded it had to deliver a mountain of reports to Food and Ag by June 30th. Its director was Martin Larson, who did more to block advances in mushroom agriculture than anyone the Twentieth Century has yet produced.

The project was inspired by the current fancy-cooking fad. Some State Assemblyman noticed that dried morels cost about three hundred dollars a pound and no one could keep them in stock. He thought that if California could figure out a cheap way to grow morels and other fancy fungi, the state would get richer. A lot of people thought that was ridiculous. I thought it was a good idea. I'm a botanist and the author of a children's book on mushrooms and I live in a tiny town in the San Joaquin Valley, about twenty miles from the tiny Valley town that housed Project Mushroom. Because of those three facts, Betty Castor, the head geneticist on the project, recruited me.

Betty reasoned that if I could write, I could edit, and she didn't think the project stood a chance of getting refunded unless someone translated the required mountain of reports into English before they were sent to Sacramento. Martin insisted on writing them all himself, and he wrote only in bureaucratese. So I joined the project to save it. One of the conditions of my employment was that I deal directly with Carla, the education director, and not with Martin.

Poor Carla got darker and darker circles under her eyes as the end of June drew nearer. The day she unveiled the joke murder plan I was in the office to pick up the last paper, planning to take it home to work on it. "Where," I asked her, "is the report on 'Options for Improving California's Mushroom Resources'?"

"Martin hasn't started it yet."

I began to see what she meant about the way he got to *everybody*. He phoned me at ten o'clock that night. "I don't think I'll be finished till very late. I'll put the report under your doormat, okay? It's got to be on a bus for Sacramento by two o'clock tomorrow and I've got to go over your edit and then we've got to have it typed. Do you think you could have it back to me by ten-thirty?"

I sighed. "I'll shoot for eleven."

It would mean getting up at 4:00 A.M., but so what? It would all be over a few hours after that and I could be back in bed by noon, with a check under my pillow that would pay the rent for the next three months.

The report was about fifty pages long, and apparently the work of the Cleveland Wrecking Company. By 9:00, I still had fifteen pages to go. I called Martin: "Come over and start

126

looking at the part I've done. If you have questions, I'll be right here."

He didn't come over. He sent someone to pick up the report and take it back to his office—about a twenty-minute drive. But I couldn't worry about that. I was starting to panic. The last five pages were gibberish. They needed a complete rewrite, but I couldn't do it until I knew what Martin was trying to say. I would have to go in to the office and work with him—each page would have to be handed to the typist as we finished it.

I left at 10:30, forty-five minutes behind the messenger. Martin had gone through only about ten or twelve pages of my edit. Frantic last-minute activity whirred about him, but he seemed oblivious to the approaching deadline. He was sitting in his private office, utterly relaxed, agonizing happily over each comma. I'd never been in his office before. It was decorated with dried mushrooms, mounted and framed. At that moment, I'd love to have fed him his own big, loathsome specimen of *Amanita phalloides,* the most poisonous toadstool that grows in California.

He put down his pencil and gave me his full attention. He answered my questions slowly and deliberately, fully and completely—and then some. I was sweating with impatience by the time he'd finished.

I started the rewrite and he worked on the rest of my edit, interrupting me now and then. I answered as shortly as I could, but somehow he managed to work in a few questions about my background and whether I'd be available for future jobs—questions I really couldn't ignore without being horribly rude. And I didn't want to be rude, but it was getting on toward noon—we had only two hours to get the report on the bus. The typist came in, grabbed a sheaf of papers, and left. Carla came in in a panic. She had a bunch of color samples with her, in shades of mushroom tan, mushroom gray, and mushroom gray-green. "Martin," she said, "the man from the bindery is here. Pick the color for the cover—quick."

"Oops. Stop the presses," he said. "A lifetime decision." He began to pore over the samples. I resumed typing. Carla left.

"Katherine, what do you think?" He spread about twenty samples out in front of me. I picked a soft gray-green.

"I don't think so," he said. "I think this tan." He held it up.

"Great," I said.

"No, I'm not sure. I'm going to ask Bill." Bill was the art director.

He left to find Bill and I went thankfully back to the rewrite.

Martin came back in a few minutes, fingering a gray sample. "This is the one Bill likes. He think the black type'll look best on it. What do you think?"

"Take Bill's advice—it's what you're paying him for."

"The trouble with the world today is that everybody listens to the experts."

I shrugged and kept typing, trying not to think about the chunk of tax money that was paying for Bill, and me, and other unlistened-to "experts" on Project Mushroom.

Carla came back in: "Martin, how about it? The guy from the bindery's getting impatient."

"Just a second, Carla. This is important."

Carla disappeared. Martin continued to stare at the samples. Finally, he picked another gray—at least it must have been another gray since it was on a different sample card. But it looked for all the world like the one Bill had picked. Martin covered it with a sample of black type, then put the sample on the gray Bill had picked. Sure enough, it showed up better on

Bill's gray. Martin pointed to his own gray. "I think this is a much richer color, don't you?"

"I hardly see any difference at all." This time I couldn't keep the curtness out of my voice.

"I know what I'll do. I'll ask Betty." Martin picked up the phone and spoke to Betty: "Get your fanny in here. We've got a problem"

I kept typing. In a second, Betty whirled in, hair flying, arms full of papers, face frantic. "What's the problem?"

Martin explained—slowly. Betty told him to listen to Bill.

When she had left, Martin stared at the color cards some more. Finally, he stood up. "I'm going to have to flip a coin," he said. "Tails, we go with Bill's choice. Heads, we go with mine."

He flipped a quarter onto my typing table. It was tails.

"That's it," I said. "Go with Bill's gray."

"This is important, Katherine. It's got to be right."

"So go with your gray."

"I'm not sure. I'm just not sure."

He sat down and stared at the samples some more. Carla came in, red-faced: "Martin, for heaven's sake. We're paying this guy by the minute."

I guess she meant the man from the bindery. I didn't ask. Martin went out with her, and came back in about ten minutes, just as I was pulling the final page of the rewrite out of the typewriter. "We went with one of the tan ones."

"I'm sure it'll look very nice. Can you look this over? There's about fifteen minutes to get it read and typed."

Carla rushed in again. "We've got five typists standing by. Any pages yet?"

Martin waved her away. "Katherine," he said, "after this is over, could you give me some pointers on improving my writing style?"

"Sure. Tomorrow maybe."

"My main problem is I have so much to say, you know? I don't want any of those guys at Food and Ag to miss anything. I think if we just—"

In my head, a clock ticked away. "Oh, dear!" I put my hand to my mouth. "I've just forgotten something. Martin, can you excuse me a second?"

I ran from the room and ducked into Carla's office. I picked up the phone and started dialing numbers at random, trying to look busy in case Martin followed me and tried to finish his sentence. I called my mother, my sister, and my boy friend, who was on a business trip in New York.

Finally I saw Martin burst out of his office, waving the rewrite pages. He raced over to the head typist's desk and said, "Type like the wind." He was smiling, clearly having the time of his life. The other four typists each rushed over and took a page. They typed like the wind. Carla stood by, playing with a set of keys, ready to race the finished report to the bindery.

I went to lunch with Betty. Two beers and a ham sandwich later I felt nearly normal again. I came back to the office with her to get directions to Bill's house, where a Project Mushroom New Fiscal Year Party was going to take place in a few hours. Betty was explaining how to get there when Carla came in, streaming tears: "I missed the bus."

Martin put an arm around her. "No big deal. I called Food and Ag yesterday—they gave us a day's grace."

Carla shoved him away and clomped out of the room, not looking at Martin, Betty, or me, simply getting out of the room quick. Martin apparently didn't notice. He turned to me: "Katherine, I went through your edit pretty quickly. I think we're going to have to do a few things over."

So I didn't go to the New Fiscal Year Party after all. I

stayed home and worked. I'd been looking forward to the party, too. It was a potluck dinner, and everything on the menu had mushrooms in it. There were stuffed mushrooms for hors d'oeuvres and then mushroom soup and marinated mushrooms and mushroom crepes. Dessert was cake in the shape of a mushroom.

I worked until 1:00 A.M. and then I took my edit of Martin's rewrite of my rewrite over to the project office and pushed it through the mail slot as arranged. After that, I went home, took the phone off the hook, and slept. I slept through most of the next day, getting up late in the afternoon to eat and read a little. Then I went back to bed and slept all night.

The headline in the next day's paper was PROJECT MUSHROOM DIRECTOR DIES OF MUSHROOM POISONING. The story told about the New Fiscal Year Party, and what had been on the menu, and said that Martin had been poisoned by an *Amanita phalloides*. No one else had been stricken. No one could explain how the *phalloides* had gotten into any of the dishes, as only domesticated mushrooms had been used.

It was a Saturday, so I knew no one would be at Project Mushroom. I went over and got the guard to let me in by saying I'd left a book in the office. Then I went into Martin's private office. His mushroom collection was still intact, except for the framed *phalloides*. Another specimen, an *Amanita muscaria,* had been hung in its place. I called Carla and told her the *phalloides* was missing. "What *phalloides?*" she said. "Martin never had a *phalloides* specimen."

I called Betty. She'd never seen the *phalloides,* either. Then I called Bill. Neither had he. Neither had the head typist.

So I decided not to mention the missing *phalloides* to the

police. I didn't want to look like a crazy lady.

But if Martin's death was an accident, the news media pointed out, that meant it must be possible to buy a *phalloides* accidentally at the grocery store. They also questioned the need for anything called Project Mushroom in the first place, and went on quite a bit about frivolous programs that were using up tax money.

So far as I know, there was only the most cursory investigation of Martin's death. The police seemed to think it was surprising that only Martin had been stricken, but practically everyone on the staff was a mushroom expert and none of them thought it odd, so the cops went away cowed. Project Mushroom was not refunded.

I have no idea how those people did it. If I had to, I'd put my money on the crepes, which had to be made individually but I wouldn't rule out the soup or even the marinated mushrooms—a single portion of either could have been easily doctored. I also don't know if they all participated, or if one or two of them did it and the rest simply kept quiet about the missing specimen. All I know is that Martin Larson did more to block advances in mushroom agriculture than anyone the Twentieth Century has yet produced. In California, anyway.

Cul-de-Sac

"I don't believe it. Listen to this one." Belief had no effect on Coralie's enthusiasm. She circled the ad, starred it three times, and read it aloud. " 'REDUCED RENT for the right person. Beautiful old Victorian in quiet cul-de-sac. 4 bedrooms, 3 baths, all the charm of yesteryear. Mature gentleman will share and reduce rent for caring prof. lady, can be household manager. View of vineyards, landscaped beyond belief. $Cost negot.' "

"You've got to watch that word 'charm'," I said, "especially in the same phrase with 'yesteryear.' "

"It sounds too good to be true, huh?"

"When he says 'right person,' he probably means strapping female carpenter. Suitable for renovating old homes by day, rejuvenating 'mature' bones by night."

"Well, it can't hurt to call."

I handed her the phone, trying not to be too cross about it. My cherished next door neighbor, Tony the Bartender, had left six months before to try his luck in Alaska, and Coralie McKinnon had moved in.

Coralie had straight black hair that blew in the wind most of the time. She wore purple and black, with deep red lipstick, and she must have weighed something in the neighborhood of a hundred and sixty but she was five-eight and she could almost carry it. She was pushing fifty, I guess, because she'd moved to the City for purposes of dumping her husband of twenty-five years.

The quarter century of domesticity had taken its toll. She

133

always had something bubbling on the stove—chili or gumbo or goulash or split pea soup or cassoulet. She was made for North Beach—and she was a next door neighbor from heaven.

Quite possibly she was the only human in the world who could get away with calling me "matzo ball." This was meant neither as a slur on my ethnicity nor as an insult to my slightly rounded person. Coralie felt I was a little on the unleavened side. Though *I* feel I'm the most casual of lawyers, Coralie thought I got too involved in my cases and too bent out of shape when my so called beau, Rob Burns, got too involved in *his* work.

So Coralie had decided to lighten me up. She recruited me for fabulous nature walks, and she took me to every comedy club and every half-baked neighborhood theater in the city and she introduced me to all her kooky actor friends. In a word, Coralie was a kick.

Some city people would give anything to live in the wine country, but Coralie had brought up two kids there (a third had died of bone cancer), all the while longing for the bohemian life of North Beach. I guess nobody'd told her the rents had gone up and the beatniks had moved on shortly before she got married (except for the random washed-up poet still popping into Specs now and then for a picon punch).

The latter fact disappointed her not at all—North Beach is still a neighborhood with enough zip and dash for just about anybody—but the former was a problem, and so was the commute. Coralie taught drama part-time at Sonoma State and try as she might, she couldn't make city life work out for her. She'd gotten a lump sum from her ex and her funds were dwindling. So she was moving back to Sonoma. She'd told me about it with Piaf on the stereo, belting out, "Je ne regrette rien . . ." (A flair for drama went with the territory.)

"It's been the best six months of my life," she'd said, "but I want to travel sometime. I have to think about investing . . ."

I felt awful. I wished I'd been her divorce lawyer and knew if I had been she'd have done a lot better in court. I felt awful for myself too. By now she wasn't just a neighbor, she was a good friend.

Coralie handed back the phone and I hung it on the wall. "Call me Ms. Right," she said. "He lost his mom a while ago. I think he's looking for another, and I'm auditioning tomorrow. What do you think? Am I the mom from Central Casting?"

"How old is he—ten?"

"In his fifties, I'd say."

"Sounds harmless enough."

"Rebecca, you don't know the half of it. The guy's an interior designer."

I helped her move in two weeks later. I won't say I found Murray Dodds weird, exactly, but he was certainly on the taciturn side and a little gloomy as well. Stereotypes notwithstanding, I didn't get the impression he was gay. Though I'd never suggest you can tell sexual preference by appearance (except in cases of extreme and purposeful limpwristedness), I maintain there are non-verbal clues. I refer to what I call ambient testosterone.

No doubt science would disagree with me, but no matter, the truth is this: all interested men exude testosterone clouds in which they envelope the women to whom they're attracted. This is true of married men, guys who come to fix the washing machine, and rival lawyers, as well as horny guys in bars, your own boy friend, and teen-agers (who spray the stuff willy-nilly all over everything). If a man is interested in several women in a room, each will receive her own discrete cloud.

The clouds cannot be seen by anyone other than the women on whom they land and cannot be missed by their targets. Their denseness depends on the man's degree of interest. If the guy's in love, these things can obscure the visibility of both parties like tulle fog.

Murray's ambient testosterone didn't exactly amount to a pea-souper, but if he was gay, he was a closet straight. He was about six feet tall and slender, with hair more colorless than gray and shoulders beginning to stoop. There was something lackluster about his skin, and about his demeanor. He was a worrier, I thought, and I hoped he wasn't obsessive about the family homestead. However, if he'd been Count Dracula it still might have been worth it to take a chance on him. The Victorian in the cul-de-sac was smashing.

It was in the Valley of the Moon, just outside of Glen Ellen, and it was beautifully kept up and freshly painted. It was landscaped, as the ad had bragged, beyond belief, its roses and rhododendrons truly displaying all the charm of yesteryear. Plus it had a nice garage to park the Volvo in, with a freezer in it that looked as if it could hold enough provisions for a hard winter—if ever Sonoma County had one, which was about as likely as palm trees in Moscow.

For the special, negotiated reduced rent on which these star-crossed housemates had agreed Coralie was to share the kitchen, living room, dining room, TV room, garage, and basement storage space—all the rooms except Murray's bedroom and guest bedroom, and she was to have two bedrooms for herself, one of which she was also free to use as a guest room.

In return for the rent break all she had to do was shop for groceries, supervise a house cleaner and keep what Murray called "the household books", which meant paying his bills and balancing his checkbook. It wasn't part of the agreement, but I knew—and I was sure Murray knew—that she was going to cook for him as well. Cooking was part of her software.

Murray'd made a shrewd deal, but unless he turned out to be some kind of mild-mannered Norman Bates, it looked as if none of my dire (and probably self-serving) predictions had come true.

I picked up a box of books—probably cookbooks—decided I could handle another, piled it on, and headed up the stairs. "Second door on your left," Coralie called.

The boxes were heavier than I'd anticipated and my attention was on holding onto them; I paid her directions little heed. Then, too, puffing under the weight of my load, I simply *wanted* Coralie's room to be the first doorway, so that was the one through which I staggered, eyes on my precarious load, which I promptly dropped, scattering dust.

The impact of the fall knocked over a picture on the dresser, which, it was now clear, wasn't Coralie's. I'd wandered into Murray's room. Glancing quickly around, I assured myself he wasn't lurking half-dressed and thoroughly embarrassed in the shadows, and then had a closer look. It was a nice room, especially for that of a single man—one into which someone had put a lot of thought. The walls were a kind of Wedgwood blue—a flat color with a lot of gray in it, very masculine and a little melancholy. The bed was an old mahogany four-poster, covered with a quilt in bright colors, a still-new quilt that hadn't been washed much, also very masculine. At the foot of the bed was an antique wooden trunk painted a slightly darker blue than the walls, and draped with a soft dark-blue blanket.

I picked up the picture and straightened it. It was a photo of a woman about Coralie's age, with dark hair and the same *joie de vivre;* you could see it in her smile. There was something about the lift of her eyebrows . . . did she look like Coralie?

"My mother," said Murray, from behind me. "She died last year."

I whirled. "Murray, I'm so sorry—I wandered in by mistake."

He gave me a benign look that was almost a smile, but not quite. "It's okay. I like to have pretty ladies in my bedroom."

"It's a beautiful room. A lot of work obviously went into it. Did your mother make the quilt?"

He nodded briefly, as if his friendly mood had come suddenly to an end. I wasn't done, though. I wanted to know who this odd man was that Coralie intended to live with.

"Did your mother live with you?"

Again the little nod. Nothing else.

"I guess it's painful to talk about it."

He shifted his eyes, avoiding mine, and I was sorry I'd upset him. But there was no denying the fact I was also sorry I couldn't civilly ask him any more questions. Like whether he'd ever been married or had any children.

Luckily for me, he and his housemate had already told each other all. Coralie filled me in while I helped her unpack and arrange her room.

Murray had never married and he had no children, though he seemed to regret it.

"Ah," I interjected. "Never too late."

She thought that one over. "Nah. Too wimpy for me. Though maybe you—"

"Forget it. Maybe one of us has a nice domineering friend who'd love a sweet guy to boss."

"I'll give it some thought."

"So back to his story."

"There isn't that much more." She shrugged. "I know he

likes kids—he nearly cried when I told him about Mikey dying. But anyway he didn't have them—he got caught up in the family business. By the way, he's not really an interior designer. His mother was one. His father, who was much older, ran Dodds Designs, an upholstery business here in town, and his mother worked there. She married her boss, who died while Murray was in his teens, and young Murray started helping her run the business. He stayed on and I guess he stayed on in the family home as well."

"No wonder he needs a mother."

Murray spoke behind us, as he had before in his own room: "Mother?"

"Murray, you're so quiet in those tennies," said Coralie. "We didn't hear you come in."

"Oh, Coralie. Sorry." And he walked out, looking baffled.

Coralie stared after him. "Bet *she* was a piece of work."

"Who?"

"Mom."

"You're not kidding. Lived with her all his life—never married? Ow."

She shrugged. "He's making a recovery, though. He threw out everything in the house, and got the new decorator at Dodds to do the place over for him. That's saying 'good-bye', wouldn't you say?"

"Either that or he was trying to make it nice for a room-mate. I'd also say she did a terrific job. I'll bet she designed his room around that great quilt his mother made."

Coralie stared at me, bewildered. "His mother didn't make that quilt. My friend Maggie Ruth did—she has the quilt store in Sonoma. Murray came in with the decorator and picked it out—after I recognized it I went over and asked Maggie Ruth all about him."

"What'd she say?"

Coralie looked at her lap, which was full of small things she was dusting. "Well, she did say the decorator thought he was a little weird."

"So did you go ask the decorator?"

"I tried, but she quit a month ago and left town."

Three days later I gave Coralie a call to see how things were going. Things were going fine, she said, except for that one time Murray walked in on her while she was taking a shower. But no problem, she assured me, she'd gotten locks on her bathroom door and her bedroom door as well. She'd call back in a couple of days.

But she didn't. I phoned a week later, left a message with Murray, and didn't hear from her. I left more messages. Murray always told me he'd given her all the previous ones. Still she didn't call.

Then one day, before I got home from work, she left this on my machine: "Things are getting weird here. But don't bother to call—I have to wait for a good time to talk. I'll call back, okay?"

Uh-uh. Not okay. Not even a little bit okay. I cancelled my appointments—fortunately I didn't have to be in court—and drove up the next day.

Coralie's car was nowhere in sight and Murray was in the front yard, digging. He was digging a hole about six feet long and he was digging it too deep for roses.

"Hi, Murray. New flower bed?"

He stared as if he'd never seen me before in his life.

"Don't you know me? From moving day? I'm Coralie's friend, Rebecca Schwartz."

He smiled as if I'd made his day, and clasped my outstretched hand with both of his. "Rebecca. How nice to see you."

"Nice to see you too." (Except for the goose bumps.) "Is Coralie here?"

He removed the baseball cap he was wearing and scratched his temple. "I don't think so. Hasn't been around much lately." He looked sad.

"You don't know where she is, do you?"

He put his cap back on and stared determinedly at the horizon. "Yeah." He paused. "Yeah. I'm pretty sure she went to the store."

"The grocery store?"

"Uh-huh."

"Do you know where she shops?"

"No. That's *her* job."

"You never went with her?"

"No. Guess I never will now."

"What?" (Had I heard right?)

Murray didn't answer, just went back to digging. Palms sweaty, I maneuvered my car back down the lane to the main road, where I stopped and sat for awhile, wishing so many unfamiliar muscle groups would stop shaking. What was I supposed to think? What was there to think? I looked at my watch—I'd been here half an hour. Surely no one could take more than an hour to shop, and I wasn't sure I could drive yet. I waited another thirty minutes, my fantasies getting more and more out of hand. Coralie didn't return.

Should I call the police? I didn't think my not being able to find her in an hour's time would make her a missing person in their eyes, but maybe it would. It might if other women had moved into Murray's house and disappeared. Or even if he had a reputation for being eccentric and scary. Or maybe a criminal record.

My scalp prickled as I tried to fight off the most provocative "if" of all: If his mother had died in suspicious circumstances.

I didn't succeed, or come close to succeeding. I was reminded of that stock admonition of gurus to their pupils, "Don't think of an elephant." How, once the idea was planted, could I think of anything else?

I headed for the local library and looked at obituary columns in the neighborhood of a year ago. I started with February, since that was exactly a year ago, then moved on to March, April and May; after that back to January, December and November—and finally, puzzled, all the way to September, since anything under a year and a half might be loosely considered a year. There was no record in any of the local papers of the death of a Mrs. Dodds. I wondered if she'd married again.

The librarian looked friendly and, better still, old enough to know and care about the local lore. "Do you know the Dodds family?" I asked. "Of Dodds Designs?"

She had aquamarine eyes magnified to quarter-size behind a pair of glasses that had been stylish when I was getting my first "C" in algebra. "Murray Dodds? Sure. Had him reupholster my sofa just last year, and two chairs done, oh, seven or eight years ago. They do a nice job there. He's selling the business, though."

"I didn't know that."

"Umm-hmm. Retiring, I hear. At the ripe old age of fifty-two." She shook her head. "Must be nice."

"You know him well?"

"Only that way now—in business. We used to visit a lot more whenever he'd come in. Used to be more of a reader than he is now." She sighed. "Guess a lot of people did. These VCRs—"

I cut her off. "I met him a few weeks ago. Seemed like a nice man."

She beamed. "Oh, he is! A lovely man. I remember how it tore him up when his mother died. He kept her at home, you know—up till she finally had to go into a home. There's not many would do that."

"A nursing home? Did she die there?"

The friendly eyes went blank, but I wasn't sure why. Had it been an odd question? "I don't know. I guess so."

"Can you remember when she died?"

She started to raise her shoulders in a mammoth shrug, but the phone interrupted the gesture. Relief flooded her face as she answered the call. I waited a few minutes, hoping to get her attention again, but she was engrossed in a matter involving the late Jack London. I must have been too pushy.

Murray, still digging in the front yard, didn't seem unhappy to see me again, but he didn't seem thrilled about it either. Did I dare push my luck? Yes; it was what I'd come for.

"Coralie's not back yet?"

"Nope. Must have been held up."

"I should have let her know I was coming up. May I go in and leave a note for her?"

He nodded and kept on digging.

I moved fast, first to the kitchen to find myself a weapon, just in case. Coralie kept her cleaver sharp as a razor blade and hanging on a magnet on the wall. I slipped it into my purse, handle sticking out just enough to get a good grip.

Heart thumping, I opened the connecting door to the garage, and saw a rolled-up rug. Thumping heart now in throat, I examined it and found no body. I threw open the freezer—empty, thank God. I cased the lower floor next—all was okay—and then the basement. The bulb was burned out.

Heart-in-throat now on overload, soaking with sweat, I searched the crannies with my pocket flash. No Coralie, dead or held captive, and no mummified corpse of Murray's mom, but I was going to have to take a stress management course if *I* lived.

Brushing off cobwebs, I shut the basement door noiselessly and checked a window for Murray. He was still digging. Okay, the upstairs. The door to the guest bathroom was closed, which seemed a little odd until I opened it. It was a wreck, as if someone were systematically taking it apart, sorting out Coralie's things, perhaps to throw them out.

Barely remembering to close the door, I rushed to Coralie's room. Another wreck—all the neatly unpacked stuff half-packed again.

Panicky, I thought of Murray's antique trunk, and headed for his room. Brushing aside the blue blanket, I raised the lid, nervous as Tom Sawyer in the haunted house. But my tense shoulders dropped as I felt the blood rush back to my face— no Coralie, no Mom Dodds. I started breathing normally again. There wasn't much in the trunk—just a couple of blankets and a plastic box full of old papers and letters and photos.

On the top of the pile was a clipping of a news story—the news story I'd just spent an hour searching for. Mrs. Dodds's obituary said she had died at a convalescent home after a long illness—in September of 1967. Nearly twenty-three years before.

I heard the front door click shut. Quickly, I closed the trunk, rearranged the blanket and stepped into the hall. "Coralie?"

Murray trudged up the stairs. "Oh, is Coralie home?"

Why didn't he know she wasn't home? Had he gone somewhere? I didn't know. I just knew I was terrified to be alone in the house with him. "Uh-huh," I said casually. "She's in the bathroom."

"Oh. I was going to go myself."

He was blocking my way.

"Aren't there other bathrooms?"

"I need something in this one."

I had to get past him, but what to do? I gripped the handle of the cleaver, trying to plot strategy. He stared at the floor. "I'm really going to miss Coralie."

"Miss her?"

"I wanted to take her on a trip around the world." Impatient, he banged on the bathroom door. "Coralie, hurry, will you?"

I got hold of myself. Clearly, if he thought Coralie was in the bathroom, then Coralie was still alive. Testing, I stepped slowly past him; he made no move to stop me. "I guess I'd better be going."

"Bye."

When I'd reached the first landing and felt I had a good head start, I said, "By the way, Murray, what's that you're working on out in the yard?"

"My ass," he said mildly, and then I saw the corners of his mouth turn up. I realized I'd never seen him smile.

"Excuse me?"

Murray laughed long and hard and hysterically. "I don't know my ass from a hole in the ground."

I got out of there.

I still didn't see how I could go to the police and yet I couldn't go home haunted by the memory of Murray digging a grave in the front yard. Not without making absolutely sure Coralie was safe. I drove into Sonoma to have coffee and think things over.

If Murray was in his early fifties, his mother had died

young. And yet, apparently of natural causes.

Why had he said she died last year? The librarian had said he hadn't been the same since her death.

He hadn't married.

And Coralie looked like the mother.

It really did sound like Norman Bates revisited, however you added it up. The hot coffee couldn't prevent a little *frisson* when I thought of the way he'd tried to isolate Coralie, conveniently forgetting to tell her I'd phoned.

The creepy memory of that hysterical laugh of his popped into my head: *I don't know my ass from a hole in the ground.* Truly the maundering of a crazy person. At some level, Murray knew he wasn't playing with a full deck. Had he had warnings? Did insanity run in the Dodds family?

His mother!

I got it. It had taken me nearly all day, but I finally got it.

I need something in this bathroom.

I hoped I wouldn't be too late.

Murray was lying in the grave he'd dug for himself, showered and nicely dressed, eyes closed, arms crossed over his chest. I shook him. Surely he couldn't be dead—I'd been gone less than an hour and he'd had to finish the grave and get dressed.

"Coralie?" he said, and opened his eyes. He moaned and closed them again when he saw it was only me. "She took care of her little boy," he said. "I thought she'd take care of me."

I shook him hard this time. "Murray. Murray, what did you take?"

"Pills. Handful of pills."

I went in to call an ambulance, came back out, and pulled him to a sitting position. "Murray. You're going to be okay.

Just talk to me." I wanted to stimulate him, get him walking if I could.

"I'm sleepy." He closed his eyes.

I rubbed his hands. "I found out about your mother—that she died more than 20 years ago."

His eyes popped open. "You did?" I could have sworn he looked relieved.

"She had Alzheimer's, didn't she?"

"Nobody called it that until ten or fifteen years ago. In those days they called it 'premature senility'. She was only fifty-four when she died. I didn't want Coralie to know. I lied to her. She might think I . . . I mean, she'd know."

"I know. It runs in families. The chances of passing it on are pretty good, aren't they?"

"I forget the percentage. Can't remember anything any more."

Even Coralie's phone messages. And where his quilt came from (though he knew perfectly well his mother couldn't have made it—the short term memory does go first.) No wonder Coralie had said things were getting weird. Had started packing to move out.

"Try to get up, okay? Maybe I can help you walk till the ambulance gets here."

He lay back down. "Don't want to walk. Want to die."

Leaving a note for Coralie, I rode to the hospital with him. She arrived shortly after we did, having been nowhere more sinister than a rehearsal of *Grease*.

She'd seen Murray's "grave," of course, and while the doctors pumped out the pills, I filled her in on the rest. I'd thought she'd go all soft and teary, but after murmuring, "that poor man," in a soft, sad voice, she went straight from distress to analysis and planning, maternal instincts in high gear.

"He didn't really want to die, Rebecca. Staging a spectacle

147

like that has to be what the shrinks call 'a cry for help.' He just didn't want me to move out, that's all. So I won't. But why didn't he tell me what was wrong? I thought I'd moved in with a crazy man. He kept changing his stories, and getting mad when I told him that wasn't what he'd said before. How was I to know he couldn't remember?"

"He must have been incredibly frustrated—he wanted you to take care of him, but he didn't have the nerve to admit he really had Alzheimer's. Even though he couldn't run his business or even balance his own checkbook any more."

"Did he really say he wanted to go around the world with me?"

"Uh-huh."

"I'm going to take him."

"I don't know—I think he's too far gone to travel."

But a few weeks later, she dropped by my office after a visit to the passport office: "You wouldn't *believe* how much better he is. You know what? That suicide attempt was partly for real—at his stage of Alzheimer's, depression is really common. And it makes the dementia symptoms a lot worse. So when they control the depression, the patient not only cheers up, but gets better."

"That's great."

"He'll need a professional care-giver at some point, but for right now all he needs is a pushy roommate. The doctors say he should be fine for a short trip."

"You won't be able to make it around the world, I guess."

"Murray says he can live with that. He said he heard Europe has all the charm of yesteryear. And he smiled when he said it."

I admired his courage. I thought most people, in a similar cul-de-sac, wouldn't be nearly so cheerful.

Crime Wave in Pinhole

Doggonedest thing come in the mail yesterday—a letter of commendation from the Miami Police Department, thankin' me for solvin' a murder case. Me, Harry January, Pinhole, Mississippi's chief of police and sole officer of the law! I figured my brethren of the Bay at Biscayne had taken leave of their senses.

But I got to studyin' on the thing a while and I looked up the date I was supposed to've perpetrated this triumph and the whole thing come back to me. Blamed if I *didn't* solve a murder for them peckerwoods—it just wasn't no big thing at the time.

If happened the day Mrs. Flossie Chestnut come in, cryin' and takin' on cause her boy Johnny'd been kidnapped. Least that was her suspicion, but I knew that young'un pretty well and in my opinion there wasn't no kidnapper in Mississippi brave enough for such a undertakin'. Bein' as it was my duty, however, I took down a report of the incident, since he *could've* got hit by a car or fell down somebody's well or somethin'.

Mrs. Flossie said she hadn't seen a sign of him since three o'clock the day before when she caught him ridin' his pony standin' up. Naturally she told him he oughtn't to do it 'cause he could break his neck and it probably wasn't too easy on the pony neither. Then she emphasized her point by the administration of a sound hidin' and left him repentin' in the barn.

She wasn't hardly worried when he didn't show up for supper, on account of that was one of his favorite tricks when

149

he was sulkin'. Seems his practice was to sneak in after ever'body else'd gone to sleep, raid the icebox, and go to bed without takin' a bath. Then he'd come down to breakfast just like nothin' ever happened. Only he didn't that mornin' and Mrs. Flossie had ascertained his bed hadn't been slept in.

I told Mrs. Flossie he would likely be home in time for lunch and sent her on back to her ranch-style home with heated swimmin' pool and green-house full of orchids. Come to think about it, her and her old man were 'bout the only folks in town had enough cash to warrant holdin' their offspring for ransom, but I still couldn't believe it. Some say Pinhole got its name cause it ain't no bigger'n one, and the fact is we just don't have much crime here in the country. I spend most of my mornin's playin' gin rummy with Joshua Clow, who is retired from the drygoods business, and Mrs. Flossie had already played merry heck with my schedule.

But there wasn't no sense grumblin' about it. I broadcast a missin' juvenile report on the police radio and commenced to contemplatin' what to do next. Seemed like the best thing was to wait till after lunch, see if the little varmint turned up, and, if he didn't, get up a search party. It was goin' to ruin my day pretty thorough, but I didn't see no help for it.

'Long about that time, the blessed phone rang. It was young Judy Scarborough, down at the motel, claimin' she had gone and caught a live criminal without my assistance and feelin' mighty pleased with herself. Seems she had noticed that a Mr. Leroy Livingston, who had just checked in at her establishment, had a different handwritin' when he registered than was on the credit card he used to pay in advance. Young Judy called the credit company soon as her guest went off to his room and learned the Mr. Livingston who owned the card was in his sixties, whereas her Mr. Livingston wasn't a day over twenty-five.

It sounded like she had a genuine thief on her hands, so I went on over and took him into custody. Sure enough, his driver's license and other papers plainly indicated he was James Williamson of Little Rock, Arkansas. Among his possessions he had an employee identification card for Mr. Leroy Livingston of the same town from a department store where Mr. Livingston apparently carried out janitorial chores.

So I locked up Mr. Williamson and got on the telephone to tell Mr. Livingston we had found his missin' credit card. His boss said he was on vacation and give me the number of his sister, with whom he made his home. I called Miss Livingston to give her the glad tidin's, and she said her lovin' brother was in Surfside, Florida. Said he was visitin' with a friend of his youth, a Catholic priest whose name she couldn't quite recollect, 'cept she knew he was of Italian descent.

By this time I was runnin' up quite a little phone bill for the taxpayers of Pinhole, but I can't never stand not to finish what I start. So I called my brother police in Surfside, Florida, meanwhile motionin' for Mrs. Annie Johnson to please set down, as she had just come into the station. Surfside's finest tells me there is a Father Fugazi at Holy Name Church, and I jot down the number for future reference.

"What can I do for you, Annie?" I says then, and Mrs. Annie gets so agitated I thought I was goin' to have to round up some smellin' salts. Well, sir, soon's I got her calmed down, it was like a instant replay of that mornin's colloquy with Mrs. Flossie Chestnut. Seems her boy Jimmy has disappeared under much the same circumstances as young Johnny Chestnut. She punished him the day before for somethin' he was doin' and hadn't laid eyes on him since. Just to make conversation and get her mind off what might'a happened I says, casual like, "Mind if I ax you what kind 'a misbehavior you caught him at?" And she turns every color in a Mississippi sunset.

But she sees it's her duty to cooperate with the law and she does. "I caught him makin' up his face," she says.

"Beg pardon?"

"He was experimentin' with my cosmetics," she says this time, very tight-lipped and dignified, and I begin to see why she is upset. But I figure it's my duty to be reassurin'.

"Well, now," says I, "I reckon it was just a childish prank—not that it didn't bear a lickin' for wastin' perfectly good face paint—but I don't 'spect it's nothin' to be embarrassed about. Now you run along home and see if he don't come home to lunch."

Sweat has begun to pour off me by this time as I realize I got two honest-to-Pete missin' juveniles and a live credit-card thief on my hands. Spite of myself, my mind starts wanderin' to the kind of trouble these young'uns could've got theirselves into, and it ain't pretty.

I broadcast another missin' juvenile report and start thinkin' again. Bein' as it was a Saturday I knew it wouldn't do no good callin' up the school to see if they was in attendance. But what I could do, I could call up Liza Smith, who's been principal for two generations and knows ever'thing about every kid in Pinhole.

She tells me Jimmy and Johnny is best friends and gives me two examples of where they like to play. Lord knows how she knew 'em. One is a old abandoned culvert 'bout two miles out of town and the other is a giant oak tree on ol' man Fisher's land, big enough to climb in but no good for buildin' a treehouse, on account of the boys have to trespass just to play there. Which is enough in itself to make Fisher get out his shotgun.

It was time to go home for lunch and my wife Helen is the

best cook in Mississippi. But I didn't have no appetite. I called her and told her so. Then I took me a ride out to the culvert and afterwards to ol' man Fisher's place. No Jimmy and no Johnny in neither location.

So's I wouldn't have to think too much about the problem I got, I called up Father Fugazi in Surfside. He says, yes indeed, he had lunch with his ol' friend Leroy Livingston three days ago and made a date with him to go on a auto trip to DeLand the very next day. But Livingston never showed up. Father Fugazi never suspected nothin', he just got his feelin's hurt. But in the frame of mind I was in, I commenced to suspect foul play.

Now I got somethin' else to worry about, and I don't need Frannie Mendenhall, the town busybody and resident old maid, bustlin' her ample frame through my door, which she does about then. Doggone if Frannie ain't been hearin' noises again in the vacant house next door. Since this happens reg'lar every six months, I'm inclined to pay it no mind, but Frannie says the noises was different this time—kinda like voices, only more shrill. I tell Frannie I'll investigate later, but nothin' will do but what I have to do it right then.

Me and Frannie go over to that vacant house and I climb in the window I always do, but this time it's different from before. Because right away I find somethin' hadn't oughta be there—a blue windbreaker 'bout the right size for a eight-year old, which is what Jimmy and Johnny both are. I ask Frannie if those noises coulda been kids' voices and she says didn't sound like it but it could be. I ask her if she heard any grown-ups' voices as well. She says she ain't sure. So I deduce that either Jimmy or Johnny or both has spend the night in the vacant house, either in the company of a kidnapper or not.

I go back to the station and call the Chestnuts and Johnsons. Ain't neither Jimmy nor Johnny been home to lunch, but ain't no ransom notes arrived either. Oh, yeah, and Johnny's favorite jacket's a blue windbreaker. And sure enough, it ain't in his closet.

No sooner have I hung up the phone than my office is a reg'lar beehive of activity again. Three ladies from the Baptist church have arrived, in as big a huff as I have noticed anybody in all month. Turns out half the goods they was about to offer at a church bake sale that very afternoon have mysteriously disappeared and they are demandin' instant justice. There ain't no question crime has come to the country. I say I will launch an immediate investigation and I hustle those pillars of the community out of my office.

Course I had my suspicions 'bout who the thieves were—and I bet you can guess which young rascals I had in mind—but that still didn't get me no forrader with findin' 'em.

I made up my mind to take a walk around the block in search of inspiration, but first I called the Dade County, Florida, sheriff's office—which is in charge of Surfside, which is a suburb of Miami. I asked if they had any unidentified bodies turn up in the last few days and they acted like they thought I was touched, but said they'd check.

I walked the half block up to the square, said hello to the reg'lars sittin' on the benches there, and passed a telephone pole with some sorta advertisement illegally posted on it. I was halfway around the square without a idea in my head when all of a sudden it come to me—the meanin' of that poster on the telephone pole. It said the circus was comin' to town.

I doubled back and gave it a closer squint. It said there was gon' to be a big time under the big top on October 19, which was that very Saturday. But the date had been pasted over, like on menus when they hike up the prices and paste the new ones over the old ones. I peeled the pasted-over date off and saw that the original one was October 18, which was the day before. Course I don't know when that date's been changed, but it gives me a idea. I figure long as them circus folks ain't changed their minds again, they oughta be pitchin' tents on the fairgrounds right about then.

It ain't but five minutes before I'm out there makin' inquiries, which prove fruitful in the extreme. Come to find out, two young gentlemen 'bout eight years of age have come 'round seekin' careers amid the sawdust and the greasepaint not half an hour before. They have been politely turned down and sent to pat the ponies, which is what I find 'em doin'.

In case you're wonderin', as were the Chestnuts and the Johnsons, it wasn't nothin' at all to study out once I seen that poster. I thought back to one young'un ridin' his pony standin' up and another one tryin' on his mama's pancake and I couldn't help concludin' that Johnny and Jimmy had aspirations to gainful employment, as a trick rider and a clown respectively.

Then I see that the date of the engagement has been changed and I figure the boys didn't catch onto that development till they had done run away from home and found nothin' at the fairgrounds 'cept a sign advisin' 'em accordingly. Course they could hardly go home, bein' as their pride had been sorely injured by the lickin's they had recently undergone, so they just hid out overnight in the vacant house, stole baked goods from the Baptist ladies to keep theirselves alive, and hared off to join the circus soon's it showed up.

That's all there was to it.

All's well that ends well, I says to the Chestnuts and the Johnson, 'cept for one little detail—them kids, says I, is going to have to make restitution for them cakes and cookies they helped theirselves to. And I'm proud to say that come the next bake sale them two eight-year-olds got out in the kitchen and rattled them pots and pans till they had produced some merchandise them Baptist ladies was mighty tickled to offer for purchase.

Meanwhile, I went back to the station and found the phone ringin' dang near off the hook. It was none other than the Miami Police Department sayin' they had gotten a mighty interestin' call from the sheriff's office. Seems the body of a man in his sixties had floated up on the eighteenth hole of a golf course on the shore of Biscayne Bay three days previous and they was handlin' the case. So far's they knew, they said, it was a John Doe with a crushed skull, and could I shed any further light?

I told 'em I reckoned Father Fugazi in Surfside most likely could tell 'em their John Doe was Leroy Livingston of Little Rock, Arkansas, and that I had a pretty good idea who robbed and murdered him.

Then I hung up and had me a heart-to-heart with Mr. James Williamson, credit-card thief and guest of the people of Pinhole. He crumbled like cold bacon in no time a-tall, and waxed pure eloquent on the subject of his own cold-blooded attack on a helpless senior citizen.

I called them Miami police back and said to send for him quick, 'cause Pinhole didn't have no use in the world for him. So I guess there ain't no doubt I solved a murder in Miami. I just didn't hardly notice it.

Strangers on a Plane

WENDELL

A hundred times, lying on my bunk with my hands behind my head, I've thought back to that time, those few minutes before she spoke, and wondered how I missed her, why I failed to notice her. A mist of Opium, red-painted nails and silky legs—generic glamour. Southern women were like that. Who cared?

I didn't. I wanted a drink, and then another drink. I wanted to revel in the situation of moving, feel the figurative wind in my face, get it clear that miles were opening up between Atlanta and me.

She asked if I lived in New Orleans and I must have looked at her as if she were speaking Tagalog. What did New Orleans have to do with anything?

"Excuse me," she said. "You must have been in another world."

She was quite beautiful, in that Southern way, that way they are. Long legs, green eyes, creamy skin, blonde curly hair—doesn't any Southern woman have straight hair?

My wife does; Janet. She spends hundreds of dollars getting it to look like this woman's—at least she did; I wouldn't know any more.

This woman looked like Janet a little, but she was younger, a little . . . tartier, perhaps.

A lot sexier.

She was exactly the sort of woman I'd have noticed if I'd

been up to noticing anything.

I murmured some kind of answer; some apology, I guess—New Orleans was our common destination.

I had already made an ass of myself, but by now I wanted to talk to her. More to the point, I wanted her to talk to me. The sensation of speed was okay for awhile, for a few minutes, but those minutes were past. I hadn't had a drink yet and I was already beginning to feel sweat on my upper lip—but not because I was an alcoholic.

Because of the fear.

I could keep it at bay with alcohol, and with distraction, and perhaps, I thought, with this woman.

I told her I was going to New Orleans on business and she said that she was too, which gave me an opening. I think she sensed in some way that I didn't want to talk about myself—at least not then, though there was a part of me that was crying, deep inside, to pour it all out.

"What sort of business?" I asked.

She said, "I don't think I can tell you yet."

I liked the "yet." It meant she planned to keep talking.

"Why not?" I said.

"I have to work up to it."

I looked at my watch. "We have time. Why don't we start with your life story?"

"You tell me one interesting fact about you and I'll tell you one about me."

She was flirting.

There we were sitting next to each other on a short hop to New Orleans, we'd exchanged barely three sentences, and she was flirting. I looked at her eyes to be sure.

They had that light in them, that playful arrogance women get. "I'm from Atlanta," I said.

"I'm not."

"I'm—" I'm what?

Married?

Hip-deep in shit?

A fool. An idiot.

Crazy.

"An art dealer," I said. I wasn't.

"Ohhh, how interesting." The right reaction; a little intimidated.

"Now say what you do."

She said two words that sounded like a sneeze.

"Say that again?"

"Feng shui," she said. "Fung shway." That was how she pronounced it.

"What might that be?"

"I can't tell you yet."

"Why?"

"You might think I'm flaky."

Flaky. This woman had possibilities. "What's your name?"

"Lele."

"I'm Wendell." I let a beat pass. "Now why would I think you're flaky?" I said, and waited for her to giggle.

She obliged charmingly, and for the first time in weeks, I began to relax. I actually felt good.

Of course by then I had had a drink, so that helped. I ordered another.

She said, "You look like—I don't know—some kind of corporate executive. You'd think feng shui's weird." Her earrings were quartz crystals. In another minute she was going to start babbling about pyramid energy. "Anyway, it's your turn. Are you married?"

"No. Are you?"

"No. Why are you so unhappy?"

"I'm not." Did it show that much? "What do you mean? I'm the happiest guy in the world. Are you busy tonight?" She's going to blush, I thought, the second before she did.

"I don't know. I mean, I . . ."

"Come on. Let's have dinner."

She was a lot younger than I was, fifteen years, probably. I loved her for that—for her youth, her naivete, her country-girl-in-the-big-city sort of appeal. It was what I needed that night—and what I miss now. What I miss more than anything on the outside, even my daughter.

How many nights have I lain here in my cell, listening to the assholes yell and mutter and fart and fuck each other and kill each other, and thought about Lele? How many more will I do it?

Thousands probably. I'm going to die here.

It all came out—her perfectly uneventful, utterly enviable, delightfully flaky life. She had grown up in Thomasville, Georgia, where her father was a cop. She had what she described as an "ordinary, boring childhood", but she was a nonconformist by the standards of Thomasville, at least as Lele told it: she believed in angels. That is, she had actually seen an angel one day in church, which she was pretty sure you weren't supposed to do in Thomasville.

So she had moved to Atlanta and studied massage. She lived with three other roommates and spent hardly a dime, saving and taking courses, some of them in whatever New Age subject caught her fancy, but some in business, and one in jewelry-making. Eventually, she was able to start her own business, making and selling crystal jewelry like the earrings she wore.

That was all we had time for on the plane, but I did succeed in snagging her for dinner.

She wore a white dress and looked about seventeen. She

told me about feng shui that night. Fortunately, it was complicated: I liked watching her mouth move.

She got into it because her jewelry business wasn't "fulfilling," she said, which probably meant it wasn't doing well. So naturally, she took a course.

"It's this ancient Chinese system," she explained, "that makes your environment work for you."

I have to laugh when I think about that now. This is an environment she could hardly have foreseen.

She drew a picture for me, which she called a "baghwa," an octagon with each side representing some desirable life aspect, like money, fame, marriage, or helpful people. "I could sure use some of those," I said, when she got to that one. *That's about the only thing that could get me out of this goddam mess I'm in.*

She raised an eyebrow. "Oh?"

"Couldn't we all," I said.

"Well, I think I can help you. Every room in your house can be divided into eight parts. 'Helpful people' is just to the right of the entrance. You need to put a plant or a lamp there."

"A lamp?"

"Sure. Or some kind of machine—a computer or something."

"How about a television? That's where my television is, in my bedroom."

"Perfect." She smiled. "Benefactors are on the way, probably as we speak."

"Wait a minute. Hold it. How the hell is a television supposed to do anything?"

"Feng shui works metaphorically. Electricity is energy; you understand?"

I didn't, but apparently there were those who did.

Whereas the crystal jewelry business probably hadn't come to much, she was now making about $1000 a day plus expenses, flying around the world improving people's environments. She was staying at the Windsor Court (the same place I was), her luggage was Vuitton, and her clothes Donna Karan. (I know this last because, in her room later that night, I saw her labels.)

Lele was one hell of an interesting person—a combination of charming dingbat and clever businesswoman; half small-town girl, half sophisticate; nearly all seriousness. She didn't smile much, didn't laugh much, but then neither did I in that period of my life.

I ordered a bottle of wine, thinking we'd both get a little loose and giggly, but I couldn't help noticing, when about half the bottle was gone, that she hadn't touched hers. She drank water instead and she didn't order meat or dessert.

As a result, I drank more than I should have. And talked a great deal more than I should have.

We held hands afterwards and strolled on the Moonwalk. "Wendell, what is it?" she whispered. "Tell me what's bothering you."

"What makes you think anything's wrong?"

"You should wear a warning sign: 'contents under pressure.' You're going to have a stroke if you don't talk about it."

Perhaps it was the alcohol or the half-light, but I could have sworn there were tears in her soft blue eyes. She was a person who felt for others, who absorbed their pain; I knew it, I could see it. And I needed a sponge right then, so I told her.

"I'm not an art dealer," I said, "you were on the money when you said I looked like a corporate executive. I am one. A partner in a smallish firm."

"You're married too, of course. What firm?" For a moment, I stared at her in surprise. Once she'd set herself the

162

task of extracting information, it was stunning how quickly she got down to business.

I told her its name. "What we do is . . ." I realized I didn't care enough any more even to explain it. "It doesn't matter. What matters is what happened. Have you ever dug yourself into a hole so deep you can't imagine ever getting out again?"

"Oh, yes." Her tone was oddly bitter, and she turned away quickly, but I saw something before she did. That time her eyes not only filled but overflowed.

For the first time, I realized this was more to this girl than I'd thought. Something was wrong in her life as well. One of my many regrets, here with all this time to kill, these infinite endless nights, is that I didn't offer her what she offered me, that I never gave her a chance to talk to a stranger: to pour it all out to a sympathetic soul she'd never see again.

"My wife is quite a bit younger than I am."

"Like me."

"No! Not like you. My wife is . . ."

"Yes?"

"An acquisitive bitch."

"And you think I'm not?"

It was strange, her saying that. I didn't know if she was or wasn't. I didn't know nearly enough about her to form an opinion—and yet I had. Somehow, in my drunken, half-crazy state, I'd started to think of her as something like that angel she saw, back in Thomasville.

"Are you?" I said.

She smiled and shook her head. "No. I have faults, but that's not one of them."

"What are your faults?"

"Oh, I get too involved with other people's problems. That's probably why you're telling me—you sense a sympathetic ear." She grinned with just the slightest tinge of irony.

She probably reads books on co-dependency, I thought. She's probably trying to kick the habit and not getting anywhere.

I knew about this because my first wife, the one before Janet, had made me read one once. Someone into feng shui was probably into pop psych as well.

But I did sense a sympathetic ear. I knew Lele would listen, and she wouldn't judge, and she'd probably want to make it better; and the way she'd make it better would involve taking her clothes off. I was pretty sure of that, but it didn't matter: I wanted to tell her anyhow.

"I don't know how it happened; I swear to God I don't know how it happened. But she wanted things—Janet, my wife, did. And next thing you know I convinced myself I wanted them too. We had a house and a swimming pool, and a new car every few weeks, it seemed like, and she had designer clothes; and we always went somewhere on weekends.

"That wasn't too bad, but then you never knew when something was going to break. You know—a car, a boat, an air-conditioning system. Two or three things did at once, one time, and my daughter's tuition was due. So I saw a way out."

"Yes?" Her blue eyes were huge and luminous; eyes you could tell anything to.

"We had this client account, you see. Well, it's complicated, but . . ."

"No. It sounds perfectly simple. The money wasn't yours and you borrowed it."

"I wasn't on salary. I got money when it came in, and I knew a big chunk was due. I just had a slight cash-flow problem, so I borrowed the money to cover it. Just for a few days.

"But then Janet got in an accident and we had to have the car fixed, so I took a little more. And by the time I got the chunk, I didn't really have enough to cover what I'd taken. But guess what? I had access to this other account that was just sitting there, so I took a little from there too. Well, no problem. In about a week, I had everything straightened out again.

"But then, Janet wanted to go to Europe with some friends, and I thought while she was gone I could assess things, get my life back in order. I was starting to realize just how unhappy I was, and I wanted to think about it. But I didn't have any money to send her off, so I borrowed some more and then . . . I don't know . . . the house needed painting or something—"

"And pretty soon you were in way over your head."

"Yes." I stared out at the Mississippi, feeling a freshening breeze on my cheek, thinking how far out of sync that was with the rest of my stale, spent life.

"How long ago was this?"

"At its height, I guess . . . three weeks ago. It went on for six months, and they were the worst of my life. I mean, they *are*, there's no were about it. William, my partner, found out last week, and he's in the process right this minute of deciding just how bad to fuck me." I knew how pathetic I sounded, but I couldn't stop myself.

"Know what I did this afternoon? Left the office, bought some clothes and a bag—I mean charged them—I can't pay for anything else, why should they be any different? Drove to the airport, and got a ticket to the first place that sounded appealing."

She looked alarmed. "You've run away from home?"

I sighed and didn't speak for about a minute. I picked up a chunk of rock and threw it in the river. "I wish. I really do wish that were an option. But I'm not made that way—I'm just not. I'll probably call Janet tomorrow and say it's a business trip and go home Sunday afternoon."

At her puzzled look, I said, "I've done this before. When the alcohol doesn't work any more, when I think I'm going to jump out of my skin, I just . . . evaporate."

Evaporate. That was what I wanted to do. Hopping a plane wasn't good enough.

She smiled and took my hand. "Are you glad you met me?"

At that moment I would have proposed if the idea hadn't been utterly preposterous.

She stayed with me that night, or most of it. I don't know when she left, or how she managed without my knowing, but in the morning she was gone.

Somehow that was an eventuality that hadn't occurred to me. I'd assumed we'd spend the morning making love, then drinking coffee at the French Market, getting powdered sugar from the beignets all over our T-shirts; laughing.

I didn't even stay through till Sunday. I was bereft by her absence, and flew home as soon as I could pack, not even stopping for breakfast.

Janet wasn't home when I got there, probably hadn't even noticed my absence. I left her a note and got in the car. I still felt like being away, like doing anything except going home, being anyone except me. I drove north and then south, and then east and then in circles, perhaps, not caring; just moving.

I got home about six and they arrested me that night.

I deserved to go to jail, I'm not saying I didn't. But I've always thought it was kind of ironic they got me on something I didn't do.

Sure, Wendell, tell it to the judge.

That's what they said, and what I did, and I guess, when all's said and done, that I wouldn't have believed me either. I had a damn good motive and no alibi, and he was killed with my gun, with my prints on it. No matter that I'd given it to him after he got mugged—two members of the jury actually laughed out loud when my lawyer mentioned that one.

LELE

Wendell reminded me of myself, I guess, or maybe of my little sister, Pammie. I've taken care of Pammie all my life. But she thinks deep down I'm as helpless and lost as she is.

Right now maybe I am.

There was a time when I thought things would be all right and maybe Pammie and I could live like normal people, but I've given up on that, I guess. She has no idea of the danger she's in, and will always be in, and nowadays, that her children are in.

I would have wished a better life for her than marrying some alcoholic gas-pumping bozo from a town no bigger than Thomasville, but at least he doesn't smack her around like the other one and at least, thank God, she's alive. I wish to hell I'd meet one of those helpful people I arrange for my clients, but it just never seems to happen. Maybe some people are destined to be helped and others are the helpers.

Things could be a lot worse. I'm glad my life is what it is. At least it's a life. At least I *can* help people.

Of course it's run by pond scum, but as long as I don't say no to them, they leave me alone and pay me well, which means I have plenty of money to spend on Pammie and little Noah and Jeananne. A good thing because Hugh certainly doesn't. The husband.

It's amazing how much he reminds me of our dad, Pammie's and mine. And more the more I know him. Something about his personality, I don't know what. And of course

167

the drinking. But at least he isn't violent, like Daddy was, and he doesn't carry a gun.

Daddy being a cop, the gun was legal and everything, but that didn't mean he got to pull it out and point it at us and threaten to kill us with it whenever we did anything he didn't like. Or more likely, didn't do something, like clean up our room.

He took me out in the backyard one day when I was six and shot Snowflake, our angelic long-haired cat, just to show me what that heavy, shiny thing could do.

The noise! Oh my God, the noise! And then my poor little white cat, suddenly just a red, sopping fur sock full of something small and light, something that wasn't Snowflake. How could that be? How could you turn something into nothing like that?

After that, I used to pee on the floor whenever I saw the gun, or at least whenever he drew it, and then he took me out in the woods and taught me to shoot it so I wouldn't be afraid.

He thought it worked, because I did quit terror-peeing, but actually it was Dominick that got me through it.

Dominick was my angel, who I met because Mama made me go to church every time the doors opened.

The way Mama handled life with Daddy was, she was a Bible-thumper who spent most of her time at home on her knees praying for deliverance. I'd say, "Mama, are you askin' God to take us away from here?" and she'd say, " 'Course not, Leila Jane, I'm not prayin' for deliverance from your father—I'm prayin' for deliverance *for* him."

"You want God to take Daddy away?"

She hit me when I said that. "Watch your mouth, girl! I'm prayin' God will make him a Christian, that's all."

"Why, Mama?"

"Because a Christian man wouldn't act like he does.

Wouldn't hit his own wife and daughters."

The earlier part of the conversation had made me too savvy to question that part. Anyway, I didn't mind the hitting so much as I minded him shooting Snowflake.

Mama took Pammie and me to church with her because she said Christian strength would get us through this life. Pammie wasn't but six or eight at the time and how she was supposed to understand anything that was going on, I really don't know. I remember when I was her age, how I would squirm and fidget, and how Mama would take me home and tell Daddy and he'd make me take down my pants and bend over the bed while he hit me with his belt.

Pammie was a born lady, though. She could sit still for hours at a time, no expression at all on her little rosebud face. I used to wonder what she thought about to get her mind off things.

I thought about what angels looked like. I was pretty sure they didn't look like babies with wings, but on the other hand I did think they had wings. I listened to every mention the preacher ever made of them: "the angel Gabriel", "the Angel of the Lord," "the cherubim and seraphim", and I'd try to imagine them—great tall things, all in white feathers. They weren't birds, of course, but they must be related, I thought, because of the wings.

Then one Sunday, while I was sitting in church, the light from this big old candelabra they had on one side of the altar began to swirl around above it, and then it split off and started to spin around the room, until it finally stopped at front-row center, and got bigger and bigger and whiter and whiter and less and less vague in its shape, and finally just—I don't know how to say it, exactly—it just filled out and it was an angel. I don't exactly mean it became an angel, be-cause I knew, even then, that it had always been one. It revealed itself, I guess you could say.

Or himself. This was most definitely a male angel, very large and protective. He had a great mane of white hair, giant shoulders, and for some reason, a staff. He didn't have feathers after all, but a robe of soft, white, shiny stuff—some kind of celestial silk, I thought.

"Leila Jane," he said, "no one else can see me."

I heard him in my head. I could talk to him that way. So I said (in my head), "Are you my guardian angel?"

He said, "If you like." And then he dissolved.

I thought that was pretty casual for a guardian angel—I mean, either he was or he wasn't, right? But the thing about him was, he never talked much. At least in the usual sense.

Next I thought, *I wonder what his name is.* And I knew it was Dominick. That was the way he communicated.

What I mostly knew about him was, whenever I needed him, I'd just think, *Dominick, get me through this alive,* and he would. He wouldn't stop Daddy from doing anything, he wouldn't vaporize him or anything, but he'd get me through it okay, and I stopped peeing my pants.

Naturally, I tried to teach Pammie about him. I told her what he looked like, and how he came to me, and how you just had to think his name when Daddy came around with his belt or his gun or anything, and you could get through okay. Pammie asked me to spell his name, and I wrote it down for her and everything so she'd be sure to get it right, but I didn't know that all the time we were talking, Mama was in the den folding laundry and heard every word.

Well, she just listened till I told Pammie the whole thing and didn't even say a word to either of us. Then she got in the car and went to see the minister about it, and he told her Dominick was the devil in disguise. He said you could tell because of his first initial, "D" like devil, and because of the last part of his name, "Nick," like "Old Nick."

The other thing that upset him was that I told Pammie what I knew that time Dominick appeared to me—that he was very definitely a male angel. I think I said it just that way, because that was the way I always thought about it. Pammie didn't ask me why I thought that, but the preacher sure did. Mama brought him back to the house with her and that was the first thing he wanted to know.

"I just know," I said, which was the truth.

"Did you see his penis?" the preacher asked.

"What's a penis?" I asked.

"A male organ."

Since I thought an organ was something like a great big piano, it took a little while to get that straightened out, but I never could say whether I saw his penis or not, since I wasn't exactly sure what it would have looked like if I had.

So the preacher decided I had, and that was another sign that Dominick was the devil and the fact that I was trying to convert my little sister to Satanism was still another sign of it. Well, Daddy was home by this time, and he'd had a few drinks, which had made him mean.

He never went to church or anything, but when Mama and the preacher explained about me and Satan, he just went batshit. But he didn't do it till the preacher left.

He got real quiet at first and told the preacher that he'd see that I was properly disciplined and the minute the preacher was out of there, he grabbed me by the hair and marched me to Pammie's and my room, where Pammie was sitting on the floor, dressing eight or ten of her Barbies.

He pulled me right in the doorway and my head hurt so bad I thought I was going to pass out, but when my knees buckled, he just pulled up on my hair, so that I stood up again, and shook me by it. He said, "You see that sweet child

171

over there? You know what you've done to her? You've rurned her, that's what!"

I remember him saying "rurned" for "ruined," the way they did in Thomasville, just like it was yesterday.

"That's what you've done, Leila Jane, you've rurned that sweet child."

I tried to explain to him that it wasn't true, that Dominick was an angel and not the devil at all, but he said no one could believe a word I said because now I was a handmaiden of the devil and one of his servants, and so was Pammie.

He said Pammie was rurned and there was nothing to do but shoot her.

I said, no, to shoot me instead, and he said, oh, he was going to, but first he was going to whip me within an inch of my life and then he was going to make me watch him shoot Pammie.

And he did whip me within an inch of my life, without a stitch of clothes on. I had red marks all over me, which was lucky, as it turned out.

But no way was I going to watch him shoot Pammie. I just waited till he went into the bathroom. I knew he'd do that because he always did after he whipped me. When he did, I got his gun.

Then I shot Mama.

I hated to do it, because I wouldn't have hurt her for the world, but I knew I had to to keep Pammie alive. Besides, I didn't kill her; I was real careful to shoot her in the shoulder. The minute the gun went off, Daddy came out of the bathroom like a hurricane out of Florida.

I very calmly shot him dead as a doornail.

And then I grabbed Pammie and I raced outside screamin'. I said Daddy'd whipped me and said he was gon' shoot both me and Pammie, but Mama tried to stop him, so he shot her, but I got the gun away and shot him.

Mama never told anyone the truth and never mentioned it again except once. In the hospital, she said, "Leila Jane, your daddy wouldn't have shot you and Pammie. I don't know why you'd think a thing like that."

Since I was naked and had red welts all over me, and since the whole town knew what Daddy was like, everybody just kind of let the whole thing slide. We never even heard a word out of that preacher again.

And everything changed for me that night.

I've never been scared a day in my life since then. I've felt—as they say nowadays—*empowered*.

I won't exactly say I enjoyed killing Daddy—in fact, I can hardly remember doing it, it was just a part of the whole complicated plan I was carrying out. I mean, no sooner did I do it than I had to run outside and start screaming—I really had no time to sit around deciding how I felt about it.

But, now, I did enjoy it when I killed Denny. Because by then I was a completely different person—not scared; able to know how I felt. *And* able to make it on my own. I was still a massage therapist at the time, but I was already working with crystals, on my way to being a successful businesswoman.

It was a time when I was feeling good about myself. That massage therapy—making people feel better, feeling their pain disappear under my hands—was one of the things I always did best. I truly enjoy helping people. That's why the jewelry business didn't quite do it for me and why I'm so good at feng shui. Whenever I get a new client, I always think they're already doing great in their "helpful people" department because they've got me. Feng shui can change people's lives, and I like being the angel of that change, the way Dominick was of mine.

After I saved Pammie's life, I knew what God put me on

Earth to do, and I knew it involved what I just said—helping people; protecting them like Dominick protected me. (Although after the Denny incident, things did take an unexpected turn.)

To make a long story short, Denny was Pammie's boy friend, and he beat her every chance he got. Pammie'd kill me if she knew what I did, but I'm sorry, I wasn't about to stand by and watch that keep happening. We had enough violence in our lives when we were kids.

What I didn't know about Denny—though I probably would have blown him away even if I had—was that he was some kind of smalltime mobster. Somehow or other, one of his business associates saw me shoot him—my guess is, it was somebody planning to shoot him himself, otherwise why would he have been watching him?

But naturally, the gentlemen of the mob didn't play it that way. They came and got me and said I'd killed their colleague and there was only one thing I could do to keep them from killing me *and* Pammie.

You got it—I did such a nice job on Denny, they had another close colleague they wanted erased. Naturally, I did it. What choice did I have? I hadn't killed two men to keep my sister alive just to let these creeps get her. I did it and I did it real well.

So now I work for the wise guys on what you might call a contract basis. When I was a kid and my dad was about to punish me, he'd say, "You made your bed; now lie in it." I guess this is my bed and I'm trying to lie in it without falling out.

Sometimes I try to look on the bright side. For instance, a nice thing is that it leaves me plenty of time for feng shui, which is my real love right now. And conversely, feng shui is a perfect cover for the other thing.

So was Wendell.

I always find someone like him. It's part of the job—establishing an alibi.

The night I met him, I did my gig while he was changing to go out for dinner—just a few minutes' work, since the target was in another French Quarter Hotel; and perfectly safe, since I was a dykey brunette at the time. (The wig and clothes went in the river with the gun.)

The way it all worked was, the feng shui job was in Atlanta on Saturday. So I just flew there on Friday, from the little Southwest town where I live with a cat and a fax machine, checked into a hotel, and flew to New Orleans under another name. That way if anybody tried to trace where I went, the trail would lead to Atlanta. But if they figured out I'd left, I had Wendell as a back-up alibi—not foolproof, but logically pretty sound, because hardly anybody would think you could really pull off a hit in twenty minutes, which is about all the time I was out of his sight.

All that may seem elaborate, but I am nothing if not a consummate professional. However . . . that doesn't stop me being soft-hearted.

I liked Wendell, and I felt sorry for him. I knew everything about getting in over your head—about feeling powerless because your life is in someone else's hands, about knowing that no matter how hard you try, you can never dig yourself out of the hole you're in.

And I was touched by the way he felt so guilty about his itty-bitty crime—I mean, itty-bitty by my standards. I've probably whacked fifteen men and gone scot-free, and here was this poor dude who was about to go to the Big House for stealing from some asshole who probably deserved it.

I wanted to do one tiny thing for him, to be his guardian angel, you might say.

So, look, it wasn't even a day's work for me to go kill his

partner. I knew the name of the firm and I knew the target's first name. I cased his office, and when I found a gun in William's desk, that settled it. I could shoot him with it and make it look like suicide. All I had to do was call up, say I had some information about his crooked partner, and get him to meet me at his office.

Then kill him with his own gun and disappear.

I was fine because I had no motive, Wendell was fine because he was in New Orleans. No fuss, no muss. Just a simple favor for a friend.

I truly love doing stuff like that—random acts of kindness, you might say, one good deed that costs you nothing, but can change another person's life. And the best part is, you're an anonymous donor—they'll never know you're the person who did it.

That's the way I've lived my life. It's the thing that makes it possible to go on. No matter what I have to do or who I have to answer to to survive, I know I'm still a good person.

I think about Wendell sometimes. I'll never forget the way he kind of did a double-take on that plane, how he finally saw who he was sitting next to, and he got this goofy look on his face, as if he couldn't believe his good fortune.

I'll always remember him that way, knowing it's the look he got about ten minutes after they told him William was dead, when things shook down and he caught onto what it meant.

The End of the Earth

She sat on a rock, boots digging into the snow, binoculars trained on the lone bird trudging up the hill. It waddled absurdly, poorly adapted for walking, much less long-distance hiking. She knew some penguins had to walk as far as a hundred miles to the sea and back to their nests. They could, of course, just stay at sea, but the species continued because they opted instead for the uphill trudge.

She felt hands come to rest on her shoulders. "Some say the world will end in ice."

The voice was so familiar it might as well have been her own. She completed the thought. "From what I've tasted of desire, I hold with those who favor fire."

"You know the poem."

"Yes. Were you thinking of the penguin?"

"Can you imagine being so driven?"

That was the day before Toby's body was found. He was their favorite person on the ship.

They had wondered who'd be crazy enough to take a cruise to the end of the earth—to actually pay for it, which they hadn't—and had looked forward to grand eccentrics, screwball adventurers. Yet plain vanilla was the flavor of the month. Everyone seemed tediously normal, except for some of the guides, of whom Toby was one.

They might have known this would be the case if they'd been the sorts of people who traveled much themselves. They'd have liked to be—and certainly intended to be—but right now they were a little young and not quite successful enough. In other words, being a police officer (Detective Skip Langdon, New Orleans P. D.) and a much-in-demand film editor (Steve Steinman, self-employed), she didn't have the money and he didn't have the time. The Antarctica trip was a gift.

Skip's good friend Jimmy Dee Scoggin won it in a charity drawing, but didn't feel he could leave his adopted children at Christmas.

"But Dee-Dee," Skip said, "why don't you just go another time?"

"Because winter is summer Down There—good God, it sounds like what's in your pants. It's the only time the ocean thaws, comprenez? Anyway, I don't *want* to go. I hate ice. I hate snow. I hate penguins. I only bought the ticket to be nice."

"How could anyone hate penguins?"

"They make me feel like a shabby dresser."

The appealing thing to Skip and Steve, who weren't all that fond of ice and snow themselves, was that this was no luxury cruise, but adventure travel. Getting there was half the trip, if not half the fun. You had to fly to Miami, then to Santiago, then to Tierra del Fuego, where you boarded an ice-class ship that would hold some thirty-eight passengers and about as many crew members. Then you spent two days in Drake Passage, the roughest water in the world, and if you weren't seasick you were as rare a bird as a condor.

Once in Antarctic waters, you landed on the continent several times a day, wherever there were penguins and scenery, in rubber dinghies that could hold a dozen people.

The guides drove the dinghies, led hikes, and lectured on such topics as Antarctic history and wildlife. They were the usual semi-loners—as close to cowboys as a Twentieth Century man can get—young, well-educated, contrarian in every way. Toby had wild blond hair, a quick clever tongue, and an air of competence that Skip liked—in water so icy it could kill in minutes, she wanted a dinghy-driver who could patch a leak.

"After the guides," she said to Steve as they hunkered in their bunks during the Drake crossing, "the crew's the most interesting."

"Do tell. You never mentioned you speak Estonian."

"Andre's English isn't that bad."

"It is so. But he's a great-looking guy."

"He was a scientist when this was a research ship. He even helped design it."

"Start from the beginning, okay?"

"In the days of the Soviet Union, there were lots of research vessels, studying various things about the climate and the ice and the wildlife—Antarctic Studies, you might say."

"Ha. Spy ships."

"Oh, I'm sure. But they did provide employment for guys like Andre. And this was one of them. You didn't know?"

"As a matter of fact, I did. While you were getting the mad scientist's life story, I happened to retaliate by chatting up the waitress in the shorts."

"Oh, yeah. Shorty. I guess that's how she got her name. But really! Who wears shorts in the Antarctic?"

"There's nothing short about her legs."

Skip ignored him, answering her own question. "A waitress looking for a better life, that's who."

"Well, in that case she shouldn't have picked Toby. He'll probably spend his whole life traveling and never make a nickel."

"She's Toby's girl friend?"

"Are you jealous?"

That was how they spent the two days on the Drake, sometimes not even making it to meals, having soup sent instead, gossiping because there was little else to do.

Sometimes the ship rolled and sometimes it pitched. The sky was overcast, and the waves were grayish mountains that shattered over the bow, reaching seven on the Beaufort Scale, something, as Skip understood it, rather like a Richter Scale that measured fractious water instead of cranky land. Eleven was cyclone strength.

The change, when it came, was almost instant. Skip was napping when she heard Steve jump from the top bunk. "What?"

"Feel it?"

"Feel what?"

"It's like the curious incident of the dog in the night—from the Holmes story."

"The dog did nothing in the night."

"Exactly. The ship's like a friendly pup. I'm going on deck."

He was back in ten minutes. "Come on. You've got to see this. You won't believe it."

The sea was as blue as its reputation, except where the sun turned it gold. The sky was a clearer, more exaggerated hue than even seemed possible. A black-browed albatross glided at the stern. That was all.

Except that it was about the most beautiful sight she'd ever beheld.

It could have been any seascape, but it was far more vivid, seemed somehow in tighter focus than anything in life—more like an artist's notion of nature.

"Must be the Dramamine," she murmured. "Or was there something in the soup?"

"Clean air," said Steve. "I've guess we've never really looked through it before."

Except for one freezing morning at a place ironically named Paradise Bay, the weather held for the entire five days they sailed the Southern Ocean.

Their first landing was at a place called Bailey's Head, which housed a rookery comprised of anywhere from 80,000 to a million penguins, depending on who you believed. Waiting excitedly to board the dinghy, in two sets of expedition-weight underwear under waterproof trousers, Skip and Steve reacquainted themselves with their fellow passengers. Some they hadn't yet met. One or two they avoided.

Like the red-faced man who kept making dumb jokes. "You think I'm getting in that thing?" he yelled as the guides lowered the first dinghy. "What if we get a flat?"

His wife was much younger, as slender and polished as he was sloppy and rough. "Oh, Hal," she said, obviously embarrassed. Skip thought she'd said it before. Hal turned to her, annoyance all over his face, but caught sight of Skip, who was six feet tall. "Well, good morning. How's the weather up there?" It was a phrase she hadn't heard in so long she thought it had disappeared from the language.

"Hal!" said his wife.

He ignored her, extending his hand. "Hal Travis, Norman, Oklahoma. This is my wife, Anna. Haven't seen you two."

"Little *mal de mer*."

He nodded. "Gets 'em every time. See my daughter over there? Dale the Whale? Wouldn't you know she had it too? The bigger they are, the harder they fall." He turned back toward the water. "Hey, Toby, you got that inner tube going yet?"

"You're in Andre's boat. Dale, come on. You're with me."

Hal said, "Good thing. She'll probably sink it."

"Hal, please," said Anna. "She'll hear you."

181

"Oh, come on. I've been kidding her all her life. She loves it."

Hundreds of penguins were lined up on the shore, four or five deep, each waiting its turn to dive in. Not only were they patiently permitting the ones in front to go first, their progress was hampered by the returning ones, for whom they also waited. At one end of the beach was a veritable penguin highway, the wet black backs of the birds coming home on the right, the dry white fronts of the ones going to sea on the left.

The bustle was continual, deadly serious intent apparent in every sure-footed step. Though Skip had been too sick to make it to the penguin lecture, Andre had filled her in. She knew that both mates sat on the nests, taking turns going to sea. In the crowded rookery, where every penguin looked exactly like every other one, mates found each other by the sounds of their voices. After a curious recognition dance, involving much bowing and bobbing, the sitting mate would stand by while the returning one fed the chick regurgitated fish or squid.

The other animals, the more shabbily dressed ones, trudged up a steep hill to the rookery, keeping the mandated fifteen feet away from the birds. On top, they had both a stunning panorama and a bird's eye view of bird life—birds nesting, birds tootling "ecstatic displays", birds dancing with other birds, birds feeding their young, and birds waddling, ever waddling.

"Hey, look. There's an egg hatching. Look—little pecker's coming out *now*." Hal edged in front of everyone else, camera clicking, about a foot from the hatching chick.

"So much," said Skip, "for the fifteen-foot rule. Who is that asshole, anyway?"

"He has the suite," said a woman named Carol, a Texan with a brisk climbing style.

"Wouldn't you know." There was only one suite aboard the ship, and it was nearly double the cost of a cabin.

"He's my dad," said Toby.

A day later Toby was dead.

Andre found him lying on deck, his head caved in as if he had fallen while running, smashing his skull on the steel—a daredevil laid low by the most prosaic of accidents. The deck had been wet, and a rope had been carelessly left out of place. He could have tripped or slipped—perhaps both.

Or so it seemed until the ship's doctor came forward. Skip had thought the man was a senior sailor of some sort, the first mate perhaps, by the elegant way he looked and the casual way he behaved. He was the very personification of "Nordic," a man so white he resembled a statue. He'd probably started life as a towhead and turned golden blond. Now his hair was once again the color of a sail. He had surgeons' hands—lovely ones with prominent veins and knuckles. Skip had noticed him often, noticed that he never missed a landing and always carried a backpack. Some detective, she thought, that she hadn't put it together.

She watched as he heaved himself to his feet after examining the body, and conferred with the captain. There was a lot of head-shaking and gesturing. And then, to her surprise, the Nordic man approached her. "Please, the captain would like to see you."

The captain wore blue. She wondered if it was a rule. He had a craggy face and an air of such authority that if she'd seen him on the street she'd have known he was used to being obeyed. Now he did his best to seem her supplicant. "Miss Langdon. That is, *Detective* Langdon. We have a small problem. The doctor here says our late friend Toby has more than one injury, inconsistent with slipping and falling. We have reason to believe there has been foul play. And frankly, we don't know what to do—we wonder if you would be kind enough to help us?"

"Of course. Let's get everyone off the deck and rope it off. Wake up everyone who isn't here and have them go to the conference room—sailors, staff, passengers, everybody. I'll have to question each person separately. Don't give anyone time alone—or alone with a friend or spouse. Get them all in there together except the people absolutely necessary to sailing the ship."

"Yes, of course," said the captain. He looked taken aback, as if he hadn't expected quite such decisiveness.

She wasn't at all sure what laws were eventually going to apply—Estonian, possibly, since the ship was Estonian—but then Toby was American and who knew what nationality the murderer was. All she could do was gather and preserve what evidence she could—in other words, follow the only procedure she knew.

She turned to the doctor. "What have we got?"

"There seem to be a number of head injuries." He shrugged. "Does one's head bounce when one falls? And if so, how many times? Anyway, he was young, he had good balance—and so there is common sense as well. Most people who fall down get up and walk away."

"But the medical sticking point is multiple injuries?"

"Yes."

"Time of death?"

"Very recently. Within the hour."

It was after one a.m., but nowhere near dark—in the South, the season of the midnight sun is reversed. Steve and Skip had gone for a stroll in the eerie light, but most people were probably in bed. Someone up to no good would have the run of the ship.

Skip said to the captain, "What about the wet deck and the

rope? That doesn't seem exactly shipshape."

"It happens."

She thought it was awfully convenient.

"What about the family?" said the captain.

"What indeed. I wonder what Dale the Whale's story is? While you're getting people organized, may I have permission to search the ship?"

"Of course, but—I don't know about people's cabins."

Skip knew nothing about maritime law—maybe he could give her the right and maybe not—but she wasn't prepared to go any farther than she normally would—just in case.

She nodded. "I'll stay out of them. Steve, could you go? I need to get started with the interviews."

"Sure. One murder weapon coming up."

She talked to Andre first. He was officially a sort of liaison between the crew and the passengers, his title being "Passenger Mate." Toby had told Skip all about it—it was more or less a made-up position meant simply to give him a job. He knew everything there was to know about the ship and was considered far too valuable to be permitted to slip away.

She knew the rest of his story too. He'd once been at a research station, when the power source had been lost. He and his fellow scientists had been forced to spend the Antarctic winter with neither heat nor light. Survival would have seemed a full-time job—Skip couldn't even imagine it—but every day Andre had gone to his lab, and had worked. "He was the one who got the group through. He won't admit it," Toby had said, "because he hates the Communists so much—but he was awarded the Order of Lenin for what he did."

He was obviously no ordinary man. He was very handsome, yet awkward, both socially and in the way he moved, as if he were made of some durable substance that simply wasn't pliable. There was something heroic about him, yet it was something more dogged than swashbuckling. Hercules he wasn't; he was more like the Little Engine That Could.

"If I'd gotten there earlier," he was saying. "If only I'd gotten there earlier."

"Why do you say that?"

"Maybe I could have helped him."

"How did you happen to find him?"

"I have a lecture tomorrow—you remember? 'My Twenty Years in the Antarctic.' I was up, preparing for it. I was nervous—I went outside for a smoke."

"And?"

He shrugged. "I found him. It was too late."

His English was minimal, but he had little to say, anyway—he hadn't heard or seen anything. All he had done was find the body. He seemed distraught and also nervous, writhing underneath, as if being deprived this time of heroism was eating him up.

"Do you know of anyone who might have wanted to kill Toby?"

"He was . . ." He shook his head. "No. No. Toby. No."

He and Toby, she thought, had been close. Toby had spoken of him often and always with admiration. I'll try him again, she decided, and moved on to Dale the Whale.

Dale wasn't really fat, but she was no lithe, perfect Anna. Since Skip herself was six feet tall and overweight by some standards, she had sympathy for the Dales of the world. Also, she didn't get along that great with her own dad.

Dale kept her brown hair short and wore no make-up, almost as if she didn't much care what anyone thought, but since her skin was smooth and her color good, it merely looked casual rather than careless. At the moment her face was puffy from crying.

"He was twenty-nine—tomorrow was his thirtieth birthday."

"You were close to your brother?"

Dale nodded.

"How did your family happen to be traveling together?"

"We weren't supposed to be. Dad and Anna were coming to be with Toby on his birthday. And he called up and said— well, frankly . . ." She hesitated. "I don't want you to take this the wrong way, but he said he was afraid."

"Afraid of what?"

"Dad. He has . . ." again she stopped, apparently unsure what to say. Or play-acting. "He has a history of violence."

"What sort?"

"Oh, just with us. He used to beat us when we were kids."

Skip was puzzled. Toby had been well over six feet tall— surely he could protect himself. "There must be more."

"Yeah. Mom—he used to knock her around as well. One day she took some pills."

"Are you saying your mother killed herself?"

Dale nodded. "Oh, yes. And Dad was married again six months later." She had that defiant look people get when they're trying to cover up something that hurts.

"Still, I don't see why Toby was afraid of him."

"Well, it's this way. Granddaddy McAvoy, my mom's dad, made a fortune in bottle caps—do you love it? Somebody's gotta make them. Dad married Mom and took over the company, and Granddad, in his infinite wisdom, didn't leave Mom any money. And didn't leave me any. On the McAvoy side, the money is passed strictly to the male heirs. Toby gets his on his thirtieth birthday, but *only* if he's working for the company—and on that date, the same amount goes to the company."

"Matching funds, you might say."

"Granddad was a piece of work. But, anyhow, you've probably guessed it—Toby had absolutely no interest in bottle caps, and Dad wanted the money. So, if you want to know the truth, he really came to the end of the earth to persuade Toby to come to work for the company. Toby was afraid there'd be trouble, so he made me promise I'd never leave him alone with Dad—and then he made Dad pay for my ticket."

"Are you saying he was physically afraid of your dad?"

She looked confused. "I don't know. I honestly don't know. All I know is he didn't want to be alone with him."

"Did you see Toby earlier tonight?"

"Oh, yes. He came to my cabin a little before . . . I guess, before he was killed." She snapped her fingers. "Shorty! Damn, I forgot about that."

"Back up a little—you lost me."

"He was upset. He came to tell me she broke up with him. They had a huge fight because he turned Dad down—in other words, because he wasn't going home to be a rich American. Naturally he thought she'd just been using him, and that made him feel bad. He'd lost girl friends before, but he just rode with it, you know what I mean? All smiles, there'll-be-another-one soon kind of thing. Last night he seemed really depressed—it wasn't like Toby, but he could get that way around Dad."

"What time did he leave?"

"About an hour and a half ago." Her eyes brimmed, as the reality of it hit her.

Skip called in the girl friend. "I understand you were involved with Toby."

And then *she* burst into tears.

"You must have been in love with him."

"Oh, yes. Oh, yes, I am in love with him."

"So why did you dump him, Shorty?"

"How you know about that?"

"You want to tell me about it?

She seemed almost relieved. "Yes. Yes, I tell you about it. You never know it to look at me, but I am a responsible woman. I have a daughter in kindergarten and a son in diapers and I love my children. I care about my children. Toby have a very wonderful opportunity to make a lot of money and he turn it down. Like he don't care about me, he don't care about my children." The woman spoke angrily, apparently forgetting her grief. "He turn it down and we have a big fight—huge fight—"

"When?"

"Tonight. Right after dinner."

"I tell him my children come first, and I'm sorry I must move on, and he beg me not to, but that is the way it is. My children *must* come first."

"Tell me about the offer."

"His father—you know? the man in the suite—his father ask him to come to work for a huge bonus. Toby is afraid of his father, you know that? He is an angry man—a nasty man—Toby said he does not know what will happen if he turn his father down." She squinched up her eyes, but Skip couldn't tell if real tears came out or not. "And now his father kill him. What a waste! He could have made me so happy."

"Why do you say his father killed him?"

She looked surprised. "Who else would do that?"

"You, maybe. If you were very angry."

"Hey, wait a minute. I dump *him*. I told you that. I am a responsible woman. I don't need to kill nobody. I just move on, that's all."

Skip could believe that. Probably, she thought, two or three times a trip.

"When was the last time you saw him?"

"When he leave my cabin. I sob myself to sleep, then I find out he is dead."

There were no witnesses to the fight, and Shorty had no alibi for the ensuing hours.

That's two votes for Dad, Skip thought. I wonder if I should just get his side of the story.

She looked at her watch. It had been an hour and still no word from Steve. She went out and gestured for the captain. "Is Steve back yet? From searching?"

Confused, he surveyed the crowded room. "I don't think so."

Odd, she thought, but since everyone was in the room, she wasn't particularly worried.

"Has anyone left the room at all?"

"Only to go to the lavatory—and we've been careful to watch. Only one at a time, and for only a few moments."

"Okay. Send in the father next."

In grief, Hal Travis resembled a child for whom things have gone wrong—more sullen than sorrowful, Skip thought.

She said: "I'm sorry for your loss, Mr. Travis. I understand Toby was about to celebrate a birthday."

"Who the hell told you that?"

She liked his defensiveness—it gave her a nice advantage.

"His thirtieth. Was anything special supposed to happen then?" Purposely, she phrased her question like a prosecutor—not leading, yet clearly conveying the idea that she already knew the answer.

"My daughter told you, I presume. He was going to inherit money. What's that got to do with anything?"

"You tell me."

"Don't you give me orders! I've had about enough of you bullying me and my family. Let me tell you and tell you right now: Dale's got her faults, but she's not a murderer. She and Toby were as close as a brother and sister can be. You just get any ideas about her out of your head. Anyway, it doesn't make sense. If she were a murderer, she wouldn't kill him, she'd kill me."

Skip thought, *You're not kidding it doesn't make sense.* She said, "Why would she kill you?"

"For wanting to replace her." He spoke crossly, obviously unable to understand how she could be so dense.

"I think you'd better start at the beginning, Mr. Travis."

"Fool board made her CEO of the damn company, and she's just about run it in the ground. I wanted to replace her with Toby—so why wouldn't she kill me instead of him?"

"Did he accept your offer?"

"He was going to."

"Why do you say that?"

"He said he'd let me know tomorrow."

"Tell me something. If the board has the power to appoint the CEO, how could you replace Dale with Toby?"

He sunk his head into his shoulders, more like a sullen kid than ever. "I could have talked them into it."

I'll bet. Skip read it this way: Either because of poor performance or worse personality, the company had fired Hal and replaced him with Dale. He thought he could set up a puppet named Toby.

No matter who was running the company, Hal had a history of violence when angry and—despite his face-saving story—he'd probably been turned down.

But Skip couldn't help but notice that candid, good-sister Dale, who'd somehow failed to mention her cushy job at the bottle cap factory, just might have a motive herself.

Maybe Toby *had* said he'd think about the offer, and not just to get his dad off his back. Or maybe that was the original idea, then he'd had the fight with Shorty and decided to reconsider. He'd gone by to tell Dale and she'd quickly squashed that plan—along with his skull.

The captain knocked.

"Yes?"

"Steve is back."

"Okay, Mr. Travis. We'll continue this later."

The minute Steve came in, she could see he'd found something good. "The weapon? You found the weapon?"

"I wish. What would you do with a blunt instrument you happened to murder somebody with in the middle of the Southern ocean?"

She sighed. "Toss it overboard."

"Yeah."

"Well? If it wasn't the weapon, what?"

"The motive."

"Oh, great."

"Hey, what's wrong?"

"I found a few of those too. But I'm still impressed—don't get me wrong. Shoot."

"There's three decks below this one, did you know that? One for the crew and two others, where I was strictly forbidden to go, but did anyhow. Guess what's down there? Labs."

"What kind of labs?"

"Abandoned, locked-up labs full of dusty old beakers and things. From the research days."

Her interest was piqued. "Really?"

"All except for two. One of those is a working chemical lab of some kind—I couldn't tell you what's being made there, but I've got an idea. Because the one next door is all fitted out with fluorescent lights."

"Growing lights?"

"Yep. A mini-pot farm. And whatever they're doing, they're doing it right. There's a lot of good-looking weed in there."

"So they're probably making drugs in the chemical lab—a little diversification."

"Ecstasy maybe. Something like that."

"But who's doing it? That's the question."

"Well, it would be if not for your faithful servant. I don't know yet, but I do have the key. As it happens, in the chemistry lab there's also an ancient computer. I mean we're talking dinosaur. You may recall I'm pretty good with these things."

"A genius, practically."

"The only problem is, I don't speak Estonian."

"But surely you rose above that." His whole manner was so smug she was sure he had something.

"Well the only recent file in it had exactly two words in it I could recognize: 'Toby' and 'Shorty.' Someone's keeping a log, I think—Toby's name came up about a week ago, and Shorty's—get this—tonight. Followed by exclamation marks. What do you think?"

"I think everybody lies, and just when you think you've got the hang of something it flies out of control." She filled him in on her interviews. "Let's get the Antarctic Sex Queen in here again. You want to stick around and be the good cop? I'm sure she'll probably respond to your charm and magnetism."

"Sure. I'll be gentle as a penguin."

Shorty was tearing at a tissue. Skip said, "Okay, Shorty. We found the pot farm and the chemistry lab. Start talking."

She stared at Steve, eyes opening up like a couple of beach

umbrellas. Finally she turned them on Skip. "I don't know what you mean."

"You were there tonight, weren't you?"

"No! You're crazy. You talk stuff I don't understand. I don't know nothin' about no drugs. I don't know *nothing*."

"We have proof you're involved in the drug ring. You know what that means? It means you're going to jail unless you cooperate. It means your children are going to spend the rest of their lives in foster care."

"No! No. You can't do this. This is supposed to be about Toby. Why don't you investigate something important?"

Steve said, "Hey, Skip, give her a minute to think, okay? Can't you see she's upset?"

A tiny ray of hope flamed up in Shorty's eyes.

He said, "You didn't kill Toby, did you? She thinks you did. She knows he was involved in the drug ring and . . ."

"He was not! There is no drug ring—this is crazy."

"Look, Shorty, I'm trying to help you. If you weren't involved and he wasn't involved, what's the big deal?"

"Oh, God." Her body fell forward, heaving with ragged, tearing sobs, her head down on the table between them.

Skip gave Steve the thumbs-up sign.

The curly head finally rose, the face below all pink and wet. "I'm so ashamed."

"Of what, Shorty?"

"Toby knew about the drugs. He found out last week, and he knew he shouldn't, but he have to tell me—he just have to—you know? Because he was so upset he couldn't be quiet."

"Why was he so upset?"

"Because Andre was his best friend."

"Andre."

"Oh, yes, Andre. There is no ring, no nothing. We find out

everything. When the ship stops at this American research station—it does every trip, you know?—Andre unloads to this one guy. That's it—just one other guy who gets the stuff out on supply ships. We know, but we tell nobody, you understand? Because Andre and Toby are . . . like this." She put two fingers together. "You know Toby. He put friendship above everything."

"Why did you say you were ashamed?"

"Because I go there last night—after our fight. I figure Andre has money now—I move on to him. I lie to you, I say I go to bed and cry, because I am so ashamed." Indeed, her face was as red as a radish.

The rest was easy. Confronted, Andre broke into a thousand pieces. Toby had told him he knew about the drugs, but Andre trusted him to keep quiet. When he found out Shorty knew, he panicked. He no longer felt his friend could be trusted. So he killed Toby, and Skip suspected Shorty would soon have taken a long, cold swim under the shining Southern Cross.

But Shorty was so sure the father was the perp it never occurred to her where the real danger was.

Andre ran true to heroic form even in his disgrace, eager not to be seen as a common drug manufacturer. He was utterly matter of fact, as if he were telling the story of going to his lab with no light and no heat in sub-zero weather. "I did what was necessary," he said, as if it made sense.

"Necessary for what?"

"I wanted to buy the ship."

"Buy the *ship?* What on Earth for?"

"To return it to research. To science! As before."

Skip thought she was finally getting it. "It must be hard driving dinghies when you used to be a nationally respected . . ."

"No, no, you don't understand. What we did was *impor-*

tant. It could solve the world's food problem some day. Or perhaps . . ."

"Perhaps what?"

"Weather . . . global warming. The ocean is in trouble. We can't just stop . . ."

He reminded Skip of nothing so much as the lone penguin climbing the hill—utterly focused, but rather like a machine that's not even sure why it has to keep running. She could see how he'd gotten those men through the Antarctic winter—through pure, plain, blind ambition, stubborn and awkward, but kind of heroic nonetheless. His innate doggedness, his absolute refusal to be beaten, had taken a tiny turn somewhere, twisted into grim desire, and turned dangerous.

Fire, she thought. Robert Frost knew what he was talking about. The world is sure to end in fire.